THE STRONGEST LOVE

ALASKAN HEARTS, BOOK 5

MELISSA STORM

Editor: Megan Harris
Cover by Daqri Bernardo at Covers by Combs

PARTRIDGE & PEAR PRESS
PO BOX 72
BRIGHTON, MI 48116

To anyone who's ever wanted to catch a snowflake on her tongue. To all who appreciate winter's special kind of magic.

ABOUT THIS BOOK

When Brenna's abusive father dies, she seizes the opportunity to flee to Memory Ranch in hopes that the majestic horses and caring staff at the ranch can help her overcome a past filled with abuse and neglect.

But as she starts her new life, complete with a new identity, Brenna finds she can't outrun her pain. Not even with the help of a charming local, who's faced his own demons and won. He wants to help Brenna conquer hers as well, but opening up to friendship--and possibly love--is the scariest thing she's had to face yet.

Will Brenna find the strength to move forward and forgive those in her past who turned a blind eye to her helplessness?

And when at last she strips all the hurt away, will there be any part of her left?

PROLOGUE

BRENNA BARRY TOOK IN A DEEP BREATH OF THE AUTUMN Alaskan air. Everything felt clearer up here, less complicated. Perhaps that was because she was finally free, but freedom, as she'd already learned, sometimes came with a terrible price. If she hadn't...

No, don't think about it, she chastised herself, willing her mind to stay blank as she marched her way over to the corral.

A large, tan gelding greeted her with a shake of his head and a wet, breathy whinny.

"Well, aren't you just about the sweetest animal I've ever met?" she said, reaching over the fence to stroke the horse between its large, satellite-like ears.

He settled into her touch, his dark gaze full of trust as he watched her.

"Those eyes melt my heart," she confided as she leaned her head into the side of his neck and sighed, letting all of the worry and stress of her crazy life go for a few moments. Right now, she would simply enjoy being next to this beautiful, gentle soul who could never choose to hurt her. Horses were better than people in that way.

A perky, pleasant voice wafted across the field and over to Brenna. "Ahh, I see you've met Buddy."

Brenna turned and smiled at Elizabeth, the woman who ran Memory Ranch. She'd already made it halfway across the field toward the corral. Another woman paced merrily beside her. They almost looked like they could be sisters with their matching fiery locks.

"So that's his name," Brenna said. "Because he wouldn't tell me."

Both women laughed appreciatively. *When in doubt, make a joke.* It was one of her rules for making sure people liked her and that they also didn't dig too deep.

"Yup, Buddy," Liz confirmed. "He's kind of what you could call our ranch greeter. He likes to make sure everyone knows he's here and that he enjoys being loved."

Liz clapped a hand on the other woman's back. "And this is Ellie. She's a guest at the ranch, too."

Elizabeth Jane laughed softly, then turned to smile at the other woman.

Now that they were closer, Brenna realized she'd briefly

met Ellie before at the barn dance a couple nights back. She nodded and said hello.

"Well, I guess she *was* a guest. I don't think she'll be staying much longer now."

Ellie reached out to shake her hand. "You're the new girl from... England? Is that right?"

Brenna shook her head. "I wish! I've never been to Europe. Maybe one day." She let out a wistful sigh. If only she could change this important fact about herself. If only she could be someone sophisticated and foreign, someone who grew up with a completely different life—but, no. She was Brenna Barry, for better or for worse. Often for worse.

She felt the other women's eyes on her and rushed to finish the topic. "This is the farthest I've ever been away from my home state, which is Florida, by the way."

Ellie slapped a palm to her forehead. "Of course, I knew it was somewhere far away, but—boy—was I wrong on that one. You know, I'm here because I have some troubles with my memory sometimes."

Liz laughed heartily, and Brenna felt herself relaxing in their company. She liked this Ellie. It was a shame she was leaving. Brenna would have liked to be her friend.

When the laughter quieted, Ellie said, "I'm sorry that your first couple of days here have been a bit chaotic. Things just kind of went up in smoke the night of the dance for me, and everyone has been working to set things right. Not that barn dance weekend isn't already busy enough for all of us, right? But, everything *is* all worked out now, which means the staff can turn their focus to you."

Brenna gulped down a ball of anxiety that suddenly found its way into her throat. She didn't want everyone's attention. She just wanted to blend in and be normal for once. Ignored.

Apparently sensing her hesitation, Ellie added, "This ranch saved my life. It will do the same for you if you let it."

Brenna smiled warmly at Ellie. *This is a nice person. She's trying to help you.*

"I think I recognize you, too," Brenna told her. "I heard you came here after an accident had taken your memory, but that you got your memory back that night of the barn dance. I'm so happy for you. And, I may have heard some talk about you and a certain cowboy who works here finding your way back to each other."

Ellie laughed and gave a flippant shrug. "News travels fast, I guess."

Brenna motioned toward one of the older cowboys who worked on the ranch. "I was curious about what was going on, so Howard filled me in on some details. He didn't tell me everything—just enough so I was able to understand that things were happening a bit out of the ordinary."

Everyone smiled and waved to Howard before returning to their conversation.

Elizabeth Jane appeared to be genuinely upset now. "Well, I'm truly sorry I wasn't around more for your first two days here. I feel terrible, but I had to help with Ellie once she had her breakthrough. I hope you can understand."

"Oh, I'm fine. You had to do what you had to do. Seriously, don't worry about me." Brenna was used to being ignored. Preferred it, even. It seemed she'd have to make some effort to be social with the others now that she was here, though. So, what could she say to make Liz feel better?

The words rushed out quickly like an apology. "Umm, I've got settled into my cabin and have just been spending time walking around and seeing where everything is. Dorian has shown me around the kitchen a bit. He said once you had some time, you would be the one to help get me set up in there and explain my duties. It's okay that you haven't had time yet, though. I understand. I can wait."

Brenna had arrived in Alaska two days ago after spending a couple weeks driving and enjoying some time to herself. It was a long way from Florida, where she'd lived her whole life.

But that's why she was here. This was her fresh start and her chance to erase memories from her past that were threatening to consume her. Spotting that ad for a cook at Memory Ranch in Anchorage, Alaska had been a lifeline sent to her from above, and she'd eagerly grabbed onto it with both hands.

Elizabeth Jane smiled again, putting Brenna back at ease. "I will do that this afternoon, I promise. I just wanted to come down and check on you to make sure you were settling in all right. I know your role here will be a bit different since you'll be working here but also be a guest for a while. We'll figure out all of the details, but for now, just know that everything here is set up to help you, whether you need to get your memories back or forget the ones that are preventing you from living."

Ellie nodded her enthusiastic agreement like a bobble-head toy and smiled at Buddy, who Brenna was still softly stroking as he leaned his head against her shoulder. "And that boy who's already showing love to you is a pretty good listener if you ever need to talk. Buddy knows an awful lot about me, too, don't you?"

Ellie reached out and patted the horse.

"I have to admit my heart already feels calmer just by standing beside him," Brenna said cautiously. In the past, showing love for something was the most surefire way to get it taken away. But that part of her life was over. She was safe now and with people who cared.

Stop being so guarded!

Brenna forced another smile and looked around at the ranch that sprawled before them. The leaves had turned color and were starting to fall, so she knew soon everything would be a blanket of white, something she'd never experienced in all her years as a Floridian.

But she was more excited about it than anything she could remember in her life. There was just something about this place...

"I think Memory Ranch is exactly what I need," she said, hoping beyond hope that her words would prove true.

CHAPTER 1

Brenna tied an apron around her waist and stood back silently as Elizabeth Jane gave her a tour of the ranch's main kitchen. Dorian had already showed her around thoroughly, but it seemed important to the ranch proprietress that she also show their new hire the ropes, so Brenna went along with it again.

"Not too much to remember, and as long as you take the guests' various food allergies into account, you'll be just fine," the red-headed woman said with a sweep of her hand over the counter.

Brenna smiled and nodded, eager to prove herself, to start a new life. She'd worked in a few kitchens before but had never been the one in charge until now. Of course, this kitchen was nowhere near the large, stainless steel kitchens she'd seen in most restaurants—but then again, the coziness of the ranch's setup felt so much more comfortable to her.

Kind of like a home.

The small butcher block island in the middle of the kitchen offered more than enough room for Brenna to work on as she prepared meals for the guests on the ranch. Elizabeth Jane asked if she might sometimes be willing to cook for the staff, too, as needed, which of course would be no problem at all. Brenna also secretly planned to have fresh baked goods available every day for anyone who wanted a treat.

Cooking and baking were the two things she'd loved all her life. No matter how hard—how scary—everything else became, the kitchen had always served as a place of warmth and safety. Now they were the source of her newest adventure in this place so far from the home she'd known. A good thing, too. She needed time to heal and put the memories to rest that still haunted her, pulling her under a bit more each day. Memory Ranch was a refuge, yes, but it was also a last resort. If she didn't get out from under her terrible memories soon, she didn't know what would become of her.

She desperately hoped it wasn't too late, that she wasn't too broken to fix.

Suddenly, Liz's voice cut into her stream of consciousness. "Brenna? Are you still with me?" Her new boss wore a patient but concerned expression.

Oh, no! Did you seriously mess things up already? Way to ruin everything before it could even get started.

Brenna shook her head to dislodge the ugly, little voice inside it and offered Liz an apologetic smile. "I'm sorry. Go on."

Liz nodded and rushed full speed back into the conversation, leaving Brenna to wonder how much else she'd missed while she let her inner monologue get the best of her. "Yeah, so I was just saying... well, I know you said that we'd just use your pay to go toward your cabin rental and your stay at the ranch. But I can't in good conscience have you working for free, so while you are making use of the facility's therapy sessions and other resources, you won't receive full pay, but you will be getting half of your wages. Then, once you feel you're ready to work as staff only, we'll work something out so that you can choose to stay living on the ranch if you'd like and just pay rent."

Brenna's head spun as Elizabeth Jane pushed a stack of employment papers across the island and then a pen as well.

"As mentioned in the job description," Elizabeth Jane continued, hardly stopping for even a moment to breathe, "there will be guests who will be coming to assist you each day, too. The guests are all required to do certain chores around the ranch during their stay, so you'll have plenty of help. Not that I think you'll need it, but it's good for those who are healing to feel like they still have a purpose."

Brenna signed the papers and pushed them back toward her new employer. "Thank you for everything, Elizabeth Jane, really. I can't wait to get started."

The other woman rolled her eyes. "No need to be so formal. I mean, my friends call me Liz, so I hope you'll consider it, too. And, since you'll be working Tuesday to Saturday, with Sunday and Monday off, my husband Dorian will take over those days. But if he gets under your feet any of the other days you're working, feel free to tell him to get out of the kitchen. He's been in charge of the cooking since we opened, and he loves it, but the truth is we just have so much else he needs to be taking care of around here that he doesn't have the time anymore."

"I heard that." Dorian walked into the kitchen and pretended to scowl at his wife. "I won't get under anyone's feet. This is your kitchen now, Brenna, and not a moment too soon."

Brenna averted her eyes as the husband and wife embraced and shared a quick kiss.

"Are you off to a good start, then?" Dorian asked, keeping his arms around Liz's waist as he spoke to Brenna.

"Yes, I think so," she answered with an awkward smile. She hated seeing public displays of affection, but then again, this was Liz and Dorian's home. *She* was the guest here.

"We sure are!" Liz interjected, shaking loose of Dorian's

embrace and going straight back to business. "Now, since today is Sunday, we'll wait until Tuesday for you to take over. But if you'd like to spend some time in here tomorrow, we can show you around and what you'll have to do."

Liz quickly looked from Dorian to Brenna before adding, "Unless you already have plans?"

Brenna swallowed. "Actually, I kind of do have plans. Is that okay?"

"Of course it's okay!" Liz said merrily. "That's good. It means you're settling in already. What are you going to be doing tomorrow?"

"You don't have to answer that," Dorian said abruptly, then whispered to Liz loud enough for Brenna to hear, "Give the woman some privacy. If she wants to tell you, she will!"

Liz turned bright red at the reprimand, but her smile didn't falter.

"It's fine," Brenna shouted, perhaps a little too loudly. "I was just planning to run into Anchorage to pick up a few things. I came from Florida so, to be completely honest, I never really thought my wardrobe through very well, and now I need some warmer clothes."

Wow, she'd only been here a couple days and already she was starting to talk like the loquacious Liz. It wasn't the worst thing in the world, but freezing to death definitely would be. Luckily, it wasn't too cold yet, but she'd already been feeling chilled. She had a couple pairs of sweat pants and a hoodie, but she already knew these paltry items wouldn't be enough when the weather really turned cold.

Liz nodded along. "Of course! If you want to run into town in the morning, you can just come and shadow Dorian as he makes the evening meal. That will be the big one anyway." She pulled out a piece of paper and leaned over the counter. "I can write down a few places you can check out that will have clothes for you. And you'll definitely need a winter jacket, mittens, a scarf, and hat. Hmm, maybe I should make a list for that, too."

Brenna smiled at Liz. "Thanks. I appreciate your help. These are all things I've never really had to think about before. Maybe I should have come up earlier in the year to get myself prepared better. My body might go into shock coming from such hot weather to cold Alaska winters."

Liz waved her hand dismissively and laughed. "Aww, the winters really aren't that bad once you get used to it. And I know you'll love the snow."

Brenna's breath hitched. *Snow.* "I'll admit I'm kind of excited to see snow. I've never seen it before."

Dorian dropped his mouth in fake horror. "How could a person never have seen snow before? I'm speechless."

Brenna laughed and shrugged. "Is it bad if I admit I'm more excited about building a snowman than anything else I've ever done in my life?"

Liz finished her lists and handed the paper to her. "I've marked down a good place for you to grab your lunch, too. It's a little diner, and I just know you'll love it. You can't miss it from the directions I've put down here... it's right beside a friend's tattoo shop, and he's got a big neon sign that you can't miss. Just look for Pipeline Ink and you'll know you're in the right spot."

Brenna committed the name *Pipeline Ink* to memory. This was definitely a sign that her passing interest in getting a tattoo was truly meant to be. "That's actually really funny you would mention that," she told Liz, smiling bigger than she had yet since arriving on the ranch. "I've been thinking of getting a tattoo to celebrate my new life. Kind of a way to start letting go of my past. You know, marking the beginning of a new dawn. Brenna two-point-oh."

Liz's eyes widened as if she, too, were struck by the serendipity of it all. "You should definitely do it! Trust me, my friend Matt is one of the best you could ever go to." She quickly took the paper back and scribbled some more on it before handing it back to her. "If you decide to go forward with it, make sure you talk to Matt. There are a couple other guys working in there now, too, but tell him you want him to do it. You can tell him I sent you."

Brenna looked down at the unfamiliar address scrawled across the top of the paper and took a deep breath. Well, that decided it. She'd get her tattoo and she'd be getting it from—

she squinted as she tried to interpret Liz's messy penmanship
—*Matt Sanders.*

Tomorrow was the big day. Hopefully she wouldn't talk herself out of it by then.

CHAPTER 2

BRENNA SLEPT DEEPLY THAT NIGHT. HER DREAMS SEEMED TO be the one place the memories couldn't reach her, and for that she was exceedingly grateful. Upon waking, however, it all came flooding back—why she was here, what she was running from, how her life had been before.

She swallowed it all down deep in her gut, hoping the stomach acid would destroy it once and for all.

He can't hurt you anymore, she reminded herself as she got ready for the day. *He'll never hurt you again.*

She told herself this again and again until it became a mantra. There was nothing left to fear, so why did she still start every time she heard a loud voice or a sudden slam? Her nerves had, perhaps, been irreparably frayed. Fear was a funny thing, Brenna now knew. Leaving the only life she'd ever known behind to come to the ranch, not scary. A man she knew for a fact was buried six feet under in the Florida soil, utterly terrifying.

These things take time, she told herself as she navigated the unfamiliar Alaskan streets toward downtown.

You've got this, she thought—or maybe hoped—as she sat in her car and watched the hustle and bustle of a busy Sunday afternoon unfold from her little safe spot in the parking lot.

Sure, Anchorage was bigger than she expected, but from everything she'd seen so far, it looked like the perfect place to get lost. *Perfect.*

The only thing left on her agenda for the day was to work up the nerve to walk through the door to the tattoo shop that Liz had told her about. She'd been so anxious that morning she'd had a hard time choking down breakfast despite knowing she'd need her strength. So instead of seeking out the diner Liz had recommended for lunch, she sat alone in a parking lot trying to convince herself to open that door and take the next step toward her future.

What the tattoo represented was far more terrifying than the actual process itself. It represented a new start, a fresh beginning, a promise to herself. Still, the thought of being stabbed over and over again by a buzzing needle wasn't exactly comforting, either. Maybe if she just went inside and talked to the guy, he could reassure her it wasn't going to hurt. He didn't need to know about her other hesitations.

Focus on the physical, then the emotional won't hurt quite as bad.

Before she could change her mind again, Brenna rushed out of her car and into Pipeline Ink. The sign was just as Liz had described it, and the numbers in the hastily scrawled address matched up, too. There was no doubt she was at the right place. The inside, however, was nothing like she'd imagined. She'd half expected to find a gang of bikers waiting for her, each sporting full body tattoos of skulls, crossbones, and scantily clad women.

Instead, she found herself looking directly into the shining eyes of a handsome young man standing behind the counter and smiling broadly at her. "Well, hey there," he said.

Brenna froze, knowing now that she couldn't just turn and run away or she'd look like a coward. "Hi. I'm here for a tattoo," she said, holding her head up confidently to hide how nervous she felt.

"You don't say?" he answered with a chuckle. "Let me guess, a pretty tattoo for a pretty lady. Maybe a heart or a butterfly?"

Her eyebrow lifted as she listened to his perfectly rehearsed line. "Why do I get the feeling you've said that to more than one pretty lady who's walked in your shop?"

"Okay, okay, fair enough. It doesn't make it any less true, though." He winked playfully at her. "We have some great designs. Let me show you." He reached under the counter and pulled out a binder full of artwork. His strong hands were firm as he turned the pages, straight to a breathtaking watercolor tattoo of a dragonfly.

She looked around the small waiting room at the comfortable couch sitting in the corner. There were a few chairs sitting around it, and a coffee table with magazines stacked neatly in the middle. She felt more like she was in a doctor's office than a tattoo parlor. There was even a small table next to the counter that had a coffee maker, mugs, and creamers. It wasn't at all like what she'd pictured.

She turned back to him and shook her head. "It's beautiful, but not what I had in mind. I'm sorry. I should go." Brenna turned to leave, almost feeling a wave of relief that she wouldn't have to go through with it.

"Wait," he called before she could push through the doors and make her escape. "I can tell you're nervous, but don't be. You said you have something specific in mind. What were you thinking?"

When she told him her idea, he nodded and turned a few pages to show her a second stunning design. "Like this?"

"It's perfect," she said on the wings of an exhale.

He gently extracted the paper from its plastic sleeve and beamed at her. "Then today's your lucky day. I just had a cancellation for my next appointment. It's almost like you and this tattoo were destined. Maybe even made for each other. We definitely shouldn't ignore that."

"Oh." Brenna tittered nervously. There was no escaping now. It was out of her hands. She'd be leaving with a tattoo to call her own. "I guess that is lucky, then." Her voice really didn't hold a great deal of enthusiasm.

All at once she remembered that she was supposed to ask for Matt. Maybe she'd get lucky and this wouldn't be him, but what would she say if it wasn't? "I'm Brenna. Are you Liz's friend, Matt? I got so nervous I forgot to ask earlier."

The tattoo artist's grin grew even wider, confirming his identity loud and clear. "That's me." He came around the counter and leaned against it. "Now are we really going to do this, or do you want to stall some more? Believe me, the more you hesitate, the harder it gets. The sooner you sit down and get started, the faster it will be over. Unless you're too scared. I mean, you wouldn't be the first person to turn around and run back the other way."

She laughed nervously. "You know, for a businessman, you don't really do a great job of convincing people to stay."

He shrugged. "I'm not going to tie anyone down and make them get a tattoo. It's a personal decision and not one I think should ever be done without thinking it through. It's not like you can wash it off when you go home."

"Well, I've been thinking about it for a long time. It's not really the commitment of the tattoo that worries me." She looked away and frowned.

But Matt was quick to finish for her. "Right. It's the needles. And the thought that it's going to hurt."

"Something like that," she admitted as her cheeks began to burn in earnest. "I'm not usually scared of needles, but I'm worried it will hurt so bad I'll have to ask you to stop before you can finish." He didn't need to know anything more than that. He didn't need to know why the pain scared her or that she'd chosen to get the tattoo in a spot that had sported deep purple bruises for much of her life. The bruises were healed now and ready to be replaced by something wonderful, something like the gorgeous tattoo Matt had designed and shown her from his book.

"I'm not going to tell you that it doesn't hurt. It does. But not really a pain that I believe anyone would find unbearable. And when you can picture the final product and how it will look, it can help to ease the pain a bit. Besides, once I get going, the area usually gets a bit numb anyway."

She crossed her arms in front of herself. "You're supposed to tell me I'm being silly and it won't hurt at all. That would make me feel a lot better."

He raised his eyebrows at her and, for the first time, she noticed his eyes were a stunning shade of blue. "Do you want me to say that? I can, but it wouldn't be true. I'd rather you make the decision based on the truth than something I think you'd want to hear. If you want to try and it hurts too much, I can always stop and we could do a bit at a time instead."

She looked at the man leaning against the counter and somehow knew she could trust him—and she also knew she could do this, she had to do this.

"Let's just get it over with," she said. "And don't make fun of me if I scream."

CHAPTER 3

BRENNA NERVOUSLY WATCHED AS MATT PLACED THE reversed image of her soon-to-be tattoo onto her skin. The ink would leave a slight outline for him to follow as he traced the artwork onto her arm. She'd chosen three little birds in flight to represent herself, her mother, and her sister. Wild birds could fly, which meant they'd always be free. Birds also migrated as she'd done to avoid the winter of her own life. Funny she'd chosen a place with so much snow as her destination.

The design was even more gorgeous than the one she had envisioned in her mind's eye. If the resulting tattoo ended up looking even half as good, she already knew she would love and cherish it. This Matt guy had talent, that was for sure.

Now she could only hope he also had a steady hand and a

gentle touch. Her head was already feeling a bit dizzy from the excitement of it all, but she didn't want to admit that aloud. Getting this tattoo represented a turning point for Brenna—a chance for her to show her strength while moving ahead with her life. She needed to do this. She needed it so much.

"Okay, so this is what I'll be using." He turned his needle gun on, causing her to jump at the noise. He shook his head subtly and held it closer for her to see. "I wanted to make sure you knew what it would sound like so you don't jump like that while I was pressing it onto your skin. That would be not good for you, and it wouldn't be good for my business if you ended up with nothing but a long, squiggly line streaking across the inside of your arm."

Her eyes opened wide with concern. "Has that ever really happened?"

He laughed and shook his head. "Nope. I always give my little demo first just to be sure. Now even if you don't find it funny, laugh. Laughter helps ease the anxiety and lessen the pain."

Matt waited for a moment, but Brenna only bit her lip and tried not to cry.

"Seriously, try to laugh. I mean it. It really does help."

"Sorry, I'm just a bit nervous. I'm sure you're actually quite funny under normal circumstances." She took a deep breath and bit her lip again. "Okay. I'm ready."

He tilted his head slightly and watched her. "Are you sure? You're looking a bit pale. The last thing I need is you falling out of my chair and landing on my lap."

Brenna forced a laugh, but it sounded odd even to her own ears.

Matt stared at her straight on. "Okay, so that actually wasn't a joke. Some people do pass out, but I don't think you'll be one of them."

Her mouth opened, but she didn't know what to say. "Thank you?" she tried.

"You're welcome. Besides, I can tell you're tough. It's usually the big men who come in acting like they're tougher than nails that end up in a heap on the floor. You seem just as strong as you are beautiful. Am I right?"

She shrugged, unable to take the compliment at a time like this. "I think maybe it's best if you just get started before you have me screaming and running as fast from here as my legs will take me."

He nodded in agreement. "Okay, it's just going to feel like something is scratching your skin. Let me know whenever you need me to take a little break."

She clenched her eyes tight and waited for him to start. When the buzzing of the needles started up again, she had to fight not to pull her arm away from him. She pushed herself back into the chair hard as Matt held her arm steady. She couldn't stop. She'd committed to this tattoo, and she was going to get it now. No matter what.

You chose this pain, she told herself. *That gives you power over it.*

And, sure enough, after a few minutes, the pain began to ease. Or else she'd just become numb to it, she didn't know for sure. Brenna let herself open one eye slightly to see what was happening. Just as she peeked down at her arm, Matt paused and lifted his gaze to study her.

"How are you doing there?" he wanted to know.

"Is that b-b-blood?" Her voice didn't sound as strong as she'd hoped. In fact, she'd suddenly developed a stutter.

He glanced toward the cloth he was using to wipe at her arm as he worked. "Just a little bit. It looks way worse than it actually is because of the ink and everything mixing as I'm cleaning the area to work."

She swallowed and took another deep breath. At least she could see the picture starting to emerge of her tattoo, so she knew the pain would all be worth it.

If she could just live through it.

You're stronger than this! Stop being such a baby. This is good for you, her inner voice chastised right on cue.

"Hey, hey. Talk to me," Matt said as he went back to work. "Tell me about you. It'll make the time go by faster. You mentioned that you know Liz. Have you known her long?"

She knew he was just trying to get her mind off the pain, but she was grateful he was being nice enough to help. "I actually just came to town a few days ago. I'm from Florida originally. And Liz, yeah, I'm going to be working for her at Memory Ranch." She didn't think a near stranger needed to know she'd also be a guest there for a while.

"You're a long way from Florida. Are you sure you can handle the cold Alaska winters?" It was amazing how calm Matt sounded at a time like this.

She studied his face when he put his head back down to concentrate on his work. His short hair was a mix between blond and red, and his jawline was quite pronounced. He had a thick growth of stubble along his chin, and Brenna chuckled to herself as she realized he actually looked a lot like Prince Harry.

She was sitting in a chair getting a tattoo by royalty—or at least an inked-up version of a certain Prince Charming.

Matt glanced up again, lifting the needle from her arm and brought his eyebrows together. "Is it tickling you now? I've never had anyone actually laugh while getting a tattoo."

"No, I'm sorry. I was just thinking of something else." If ever there was a time to be thankful people couldn't read thoughts, this was it.

She watched him go back to work, concentrating carefully on what he was doing. Normally she was attracted to men with dark hair and brooding looks, but Matt wasn't at all like that. He looked more like someone who liked to laugh and have fun but who also had a more serious side of himself tucked away. She wasn't quite sure how she could tell all of that just from looking at him, but somehow, she just knew.

Could he tell certain things about her, too? Oh, she hoped not.

Still, as she continued to watch, she found herself wishing she knew more about Matt. He'd already proven he was a nice guy, but she knew very well that niceness could turn to cruelty at the slightest provocation. She'd seen it all too often with her father.

Giving her head a shake, she attempted to still her thoughts and make her mind as blank as the untouched skin on her opposite arm. Being attracted to Matt just wasn't an option. Being attracted to *any man* couldn't be part of her life. That would only lead to problems she never wanted to go through again.

You've already proved you're brave. Now don't be reckless.

Matt might have been cute, and he might have seemed like someone she could enjoy being around, but Brenna would never trust any man enough to let him get close to her.

Not again.

Not ever.

CHAPTER 4

BRENNA SHIFTED HER ARM GENTLY FROM SIDE TO SIDE, admiring the way her new tattoo caught and played with the light. It was still a little sore, but she was surprised how quickly the redness had begun to fade. Now she would forever have this little reminder of her strength and ability to fly forward to a new life hidden just above her elbow.

No more bruises. Only beauty.

She carefully pulled on her new jacket and stepped outside her cabin into the crisp fall air. The wind had picked up after the sunset earlier, giving the sky a chill she wasn't used to but that she liked all the same. This strange new environment was already doing wonders for her soul, and it hadn't even snowed yet.

A soft whinny sounded from the pen where she'd met

Buddy earlier in the week. She made her way down the path toward him, eager to be able to see him again. Since Sunday evening after getting her tattoo she'd been kept busy working as she learned the ropes and settled in to her new routine. There hadn't been a lot of time to walk down to the horses although Liz had taken her around, shown her where everything was, and introduced her to some of the people caring for the land and horses.

The horses were her favorite part of the ranch, unquestionably. Maybe her next tattoo could be in their likeness. Less than a week before she'd been terrified when faced with the needle, and now she was already planning to return for a second bit of ink!

Matt had been so gentle and caring—and funny, even though she hadn't dared admit that to him. More than once in the past week she'd recalled his messy strawberry hair and glinting blue eyes, his warm, reassuring smile. What was it about him that kept her thoughts returning to him again and again?

She could honestly say the beginnings of such an obvious crush hadn't happened to her before. She'd learned young that men were dangerous, how easily they could hurt you. Falling in love hadn't been good for her mother, and it wouldn't be good for her, either.

Brenna laughed at herself and shook her head. *You don't*

even know if he's single. Or if he'd even be interested in someone like you! Stop assuming.

Besides, weren't tattoo artists and guys like him normally attracted to similarly inked up girls with dark hair and bright lipstick anyway? Those beauties were nothing like her with her stringy blonde hair and absence of makeup. Brenna would much rather fade into the background than call attention to herself when given the choice. Too often, though, it seemed she didn't have one.

Not that any of this mattered in the grand scheme of things. She hadn't come all the way to Alaska to nab a boyfriend. She'd come here to find herself and a way to move past the memories that wouldn't let go of her.

She closed her eyes for a moment and breathed mindfully as her new ranch therapist had taught her, trying to push away the thoughts that always tried to come through as she remembered her past.

She placed a delicate hand on the inside of her arm where her new tattoo lived. It would be a constant reminder of her new start.

When she opened her eyes again, a tomboyish brunette approached with a friendly smile and an animated wave. "You're Brenna, right? We were introduced the other day but I'm not sure if you remember me. I'm Kate. I work in the stables taking care of the horses and anything else that needs doing."

Brenna smiled at the woman who now leaned against the fence facing her. She wore a wool hat and had a scarf wrapped high and tight around her neck.

Buddy was right beside her and he came over to nudge at Brenna's hand. She laughed and gave the horse some attention. "Buddy sure does enjoy being doted on, doesn't he?"

"You have no idea. He's got to be the biggest sap of a horse I've ever known. Still, he's so sweet you can't help but love him." Kate reached up and rubbed at Buddy's back while Brenna continued to pet his neck. She was almost sure she saw his eyes close briefly as he relished in their touch.

"Do you ride?" Kate moved a bit to the side and leaned against the fence post.

"I have before, but it was a long time ago. My mom used to work at a stable outside of our town, and my sister and I tagged along whenever we could." Brenna continued to rub at Buddy's neck as the memories from her past flooded her awareness.

The times in the stables with her mom had been the only thing that had saved her. It had been so long ago and lasted for less than a year, but it was also the only place she could be away from *him*. Her father hated horses and eventually made her mom quit her job, preferring to keep her confined to the house without any outside contact. The only sanctuary Brenna had away from the shouting and the fighting had been taken from her.

And, after that, everything had gotten a hundred times worse.

Kate nodded. "I can tell you feel at ease around the horses. Some guests take quite a bit longer to get comfortable. I'm sure the rest will come back to you soon. Riding a horse is like, well, riding a bike! When you're ready to go for a ride around the property, just let me know. I'd be more than happy to saddle Buddy here up for you and take you out to show you the sights. For the first trip out, we do always ask that you take one of us along with you to make sure you don't get lost and so we can point out all of the trails for you to use."

Brenna thought for a moment before agreeing. "I'd love the chance to go out for a ride. The only days I could likely go would be Sunday or Monday, though, since I'll be working in the kitchen every other day." Kate was a bit goofy, but she seemed nice enough—and Brenna definitely preferred the company of another woman to that of a man, no matter how trustworthy he might seem.

"That's fine with me. I'm here just about every day anyway." Kate pushed herself away from the fence. "Now, I'll let you be alone so you can visit with Buddy here. I need to get back in and start settling some of the others in the barn for the night. I just wanted to come over and say hello, welcome you to the ranch. It's nice to have another woman around here to work with. Sometimes hanging out with all of these cowboys can be a bit tiring."

Kate laughed as she turned to walk back toward the barn. "See ya later, Brenna. We'll be seeing much more of each other soon. I'm sure of it."

"Bye." Brenna watched the woman walk away, smiling to herself. It had been so long since she had made a real friend. Would Kate be the first of many?

Growing up, she'd never wanted anyone to ever get to close in case they saw the reality of what her life was. So she'd kept her shame to herself, locking others out and locking herself and her sister in. It was going to be a challenge for her to reverse years of behavior, but she knew she had to try.

Kate would be a good first.

That was when Matt's bright blue eyes popped back into her head again. When he'd looked at her, it was as though he knew she was damaged and that he would need to be tender. But surely, she must have imagined that. How could he have known anything about her from that brief time sitting in his chair?

Befriending Kate would be much easier, much safer. So why couldn't she let Matt go?

She wasn't sure what it was about that man, but he'd somehow managed to get into her mind and wouldn't leave.

It's because of the tattoo, that's all. It's important to you, and you're accidentally assigning that importance to Matt. He's just a guy. Don't lose your head.

And especially don't lose your heart.

CHAPTER 5

BRENNA'S FIRST MONTH ON THE RANCH PROVED TO BE EVEN more wonderful than she'd expected. In addition to feeling confident with her work in the kitchen, she was also enjoying the chance to meet the guests and staff members who stopped in for treats and a friendly chat. Liz and Dorian were the best bosses she could have ever hoped for, and she even liked her new therapist, too. Though her treatment cut deep into her pay, Brenna still felt rich with life and with the possibilities of what might come next for her.

Today, for example, she'd made arrangements with Kate to take her out for a ride. Brenna had made time to visit Buddy every day and had fallen hopelessly in love with the gentle gelding. She couldn't wait to get back in the saddle and felt guilty it had taken her so long to find the time to do so. Still, it had been important to her to get her bearings in the kitchen and make sure she had mastered her new job before she took any additional time for herself.

After finishing up a quick batch of chores, she was ready to go. Before she could fully pull her coat over her shoulders, however, Brenna's phone interrupted her. She glanced down at the screen and frowned.

Mom.

Guilt twinged in her chest as she debated not answering. She'd come here to heal, yet her mother was the realest and most constant reminder of all she had suffered. Her mother had suffered, too, of course, but that only added to the discomfort in speaking with her.

Brenna never knew what to say anymore, especially because sometimes her mom talked about missing him. For all his faults, for all the damage he'd done, she'd somehow managed to hang onto love!

The phone clicked over to voicemail. Just as Brenna thought she was off the hook, it rang again. She'd have to take the call eventually. It might as well be now when she had an excuse to end the call early and a pleasant afternoon planned for after.

"Hey, Mom," she said, already out of breath from the emotional effort of picking up the phone.

Her mother sounded surprised to have gotten a hold of her. "Brenna, I'm so glad you answered. I was hoping you'd call once you got settled in up there, but I know you've probably been super busy."

"Yeah," she hedged. How much did she have to say? How much did she have to give when it felt like she'd already lost so much?

"How do you like Alaska?" Her mom's side of the conversation felt equally stilted, but at least she was trying. Why couldn't Brenna try harder, too? Why couldn't she just forgive and forget? Oh, if only she could forget.

"It's good," she said, trying to inject a bit of enthusiasm into her voice. "It's exactly how I'd pictured it to be."

"I just..." The other woman hesitated for a moment, and Brenna instantly knew she wanted to talk about it, about *him*. She'd been avoiding calling or even texting her mom for precisely this reason. "I wish you wouldn't have gone so far away. As family, we need each other now more than ever."

That's exactly why I had to go, she thought but didn't say aloud.

Brenna swallowed hard and sat down on the edge of her bed. Her small cabin had just a bed, a chair for reading beside a small fireplace, a bathroom, and a kitchenette. It was perfect and already felt more like home than anywhere she'd ever lived before.

Her mother was waiting for an answer. She needed to say something.

"It won't be forever," she choked out at last, although a very large part of her hoped it would be, hoped that leaving behind Florida would leave behind all the terrible memories she'd formed there.

"And I'm here because I needed something..." She thought very carefully about how to phrase this in a way that wouldn't lead to more tears, more probing questions. "Something different to help me move forward again."

"Different doesn't mean moving thousands of miles away," her mother said softly.

"Well, I'm already here, so there's no point in arguing about it. Besides, I like it." *And,* she added to herself, *he took away my childhood; I'm not letting that man have any more days of my life. Not if I can help it.*

The phone was quiet for a moment, and Brenna could picture her mom sitting and chewing on her lip as she fought back tears. That was something they both did—and often.

"Do you still blame me for what happened?" she squeaked out.

"No, I don't blame anyone but him. Not anymore. Besides, he hurt you, too. I'm just glad he never laid a hand on Olivia," she said, and that was the greatest consolation— her father had channeled his anger so fully at Brenna and her mother that he'd left her little sister alone.

As much as her mother didn't like admitting what they'd

been through together, Brenna also knew she blamed herself. If only she'd been a better wife, more obedient, anticipated his needs better, then, then, then...

Then nothing. He still would have been a monster who'd hurt his family at every turn.

Her mom had been shouldering the guilt for all the years of abuse their family had withstood at her father's hands. And it killed Brenna to see her so broken down. She'd tried helping her mom, begging her to see someone who specialized in this sort of thing, but every plea had fallen on deaf ears. That's when Brenna knew she had to leave, had to get as far away as she possibly could.

It was the only way she stood a chance.

She hoped that if she got help to overcome her own trauma she could someday go back and help her mom get through hers. Even her little sister, who had remained unbattered, was still hurting, too. They'd all been through the ringer and were now having a near impossible time straightening themselves out.

Almost a year had passed since he died and the curse had been broken. The princesses were free to leave the tower of their imprisonment. Still, his legacy of hurt lingered, dragged them down each and every day. Even though she was no longer confined, Brenna knew if she didn't do something to truly save herself, it would be too late for any kind of happy ending.

Sometimes she wondered if she'd waited too long to seek help, if it wasn't already too late.

Then she had a thought. "Mom, I'm about to go out for a ride. Maybe you should try to make some time to go out to the stables where you used to work. I know if you could just be around horses again, your own heart could start to heal. Since I've been here and had the chance to be out around horses again, I've felt a sense of peace that I don't think I've felt since the days I spent out at the stables with you. Think about it, okay?"

Her mother sighed. "I will, Brenna. But I just don't know if I could show myself back out there. After everything that has happened and now that everyone knows the truth, I think maybe it's time for me to go somewhere far away, too."

"No one's as hard on us as we are on ourselves. We have to fight for what we want or we aren't going to get it." She'd learned both of these things from her new therapist and suddenly needed her mom to know them, too.

She heard her mom swallow on the other end of the line. "I'm so tired of fighting. Besides, it's too late for me."

Brenna had to fight back tears. Why was her mother giving up when she'd only just gotten the chance at a new life? Why didn't she care enough about herself to try? "Mom," she warned, "don't talk like that."

Her mother's voice came out small and shaky, and

Brenna had to strain to hear her. "I wish I could be as strong as you, Brenna. But I never have been."

And I never will be either—the unspoken words hung between them.

"Mom, you're stronger than you know, and sometimes being strong means asking for help when you need it," she pointed out, hoping her words were hitting the mark.

The pain and hurt from the years of abuse started to seep back into Brenna's consciousness—her mother crying in the corner as she shielded Olivia in her arms; her mother with a broken arm; a black eye; a torn dress. So much hurting. She needed to get away from it.

"I have to go," she said abruptly. "I'll call you soon."

Saying her goodbyes to her mother was hard. She missed her so much, and even though she avoided her calls, a part of Brenna still desperately wanted to race back to Florida to be with her again. To see if she could help even though she hadn't been able to before.

She'd tried all that before. The only thing she hadn't tried was fixing herself first, being an example of the new happiness healing could provide. The wounds on her body had long since healed. Now it was time to fix the damage that had been done to her heart.

CHAPTER 6

BRENNA TOOK A FEW MOMENTS TO STEADY HER BREATHING after her call with her mother. The last thing she needed was Kate canceling their ride due to Brenna's encroaching panic attack. She pictured her tattoo, those three little birds taking flight. Her mother was one of them, and so was her sister. But first Brenna had to lead the way for all of them.

And she would.

She was bigger than what had happened to her. She was bigger than this panic attack, too.

Feeling better, she burst out into the bright world outside. The frigid fall air hit her in the face with a whoosh. Foolishly, Brenna had assumed a sunny day would also mean a pleasantly warm one. Okay, so maybe she still had a long way to go before understanding how the weather worked up here. Regardless, a cold day could still be a pleasant one. Perhaps she'd finally get to partake in her first snow.

She smiled as she shoved her gloves onto her hands, thankful she'd remembered to tuck them into her jacket pockets. This would be a good day. Yes, it would be.

As Brenna came up to the edge of the wooden fence around the pen where Buddy stood, she looked around to see if she could spot her missing instructor. Finally finding Kate near the far side of the stable, she crawled through the wooden slats and made her way over to join her. The other woman had promised her a ride yesterday when she had stopped by the kitchen for one of Brenna's now famous fruit muffins.

"Hi!" she called, traipsing quickly across the terrain in her new boots. "Sorry I'm late but my mom called. You know what moms are like once they get you on the phone."

Kate gave her a wistful smile and nodded slowly. "Well, be thankful you have her to talk to. You never know when that will be gone."

Brenna sensed a deep sadness behind Kate's words. Suddenly feeling guilty for bringing it up, she tried to change the subject. "So where will we ride to today?"

"I was actually going to come up and tell you that I can't go now. Unfortunately, something has come up at home and I need to go take care of it. I'm really sorry. If you still want to go, I'm sure we can find someone around here who'd be more than happy to take you. I was looking so forward to being able to spend some time with someone who isn't full of testosterone for a change." Kate's sentence lingered in a way that suggested unspoken words were being held back.

Brenna tried to hide her disappointment. She'd been so excited to go for a ride, but she didn't really feel like she knew any of the other staff well enough to ask them to take her. Still, she could tell Kate felt bad about having to cancel and that something else was bothering her as well. But Brenna didn't want to pry. She hated it when people did that to her.

"Oh, it's no big deal," she said, waving a hand dismissively. "I'm sure there are a million other things I should be doing today anyway." She knew there was absolutely nothing else on her to do list except maybe a quick load of laundry. But she'd say whatever she needed to assuage her new friend's guilt.

"Thanks for understanding." Kate rushed forward to hug her, but Brenna took a giant leap back. Kate's face crumpled, and she hugged her arms around herself instead. "I'm so sorry. I didn't mean to make you uncomfortable."

"I'm sorry. I shouldn't have done that. It's just—"

Kate shook her head adamantly. "Stop, you don't have to say anything. I know a lot of the guests have rocky pasts. I overstepped.

Brenna took a deep breath and moved forward to wrap

her arms around the other woman. *There. This is a gentle touch. A nice touch. See, it's not so bad.*

From over Kate's shoulder, she saw a familiar form exit the stables. It was the same one she'd been envisioning all month, but it wasn't supposed to be here. Not at the ranch. Not in her safe space. Not seeing her yet, Matt made his way over to a black horse that stood next to the fence and started brushing him down.

"Why is Matt Sanders here?" she whispered, watching him carefully.

Kate turned abruptly, which was exactly what Brenna hadn't wanted to happen. "Oh, Matt is a friend of Liz and Dorian's via Sofia and Hunter. It's a long story and a good one! You should have him tell it to you sometime. Hey, didn't you just get up here from the lower forty-eight like less than a month ago? How do you know Matt already?"

"He did my tattoo a little bit after I first arrived," Brenna explained patiently. "But he never said—"

Kate clapped her hands together excitedly. "Hey, since you already know him, he'd be the perfect one to take my place! He knows all of the trails around here. Matt, over here!"

Before Brenna could stop her, Kate was calling Matt's name and waving wildly with both arms.

He turned to greet them and, even from far away, Brenna could see his face light up in a smile when he saw her. Well, he could have been smiling at Kate, too, but it was nice to pretend it was all for her. Just why that was, she couldn't guess. *Just say no! Just say no!*

Matt walked over and grinned down at her. She hadn't realized how tall he was. "Brenna, I was hoping I'd get the chance to see you while I was here. How's the tattoo healing? Have you been applying the balm I gave you?"

She tried to get her racing heart back under control. She was acting like a silly schoolgirl whose crush just walked up to her locker.

"You said I only had to apply it for the first two weeks. Did I do something wrong? Do you want to look at it?" Perhaps if she kept everything strictly business, she could get out of this mortifying, confusing situation with her dignity intact.

He just shook his head. "Oh, you're right. Time flies, especially this time of the year when the days get so short. If you're feeling good and it's looking good, then you should be A-Okay."

"I've been good, I promise." She laughed at how he pretended to be so serious. *Stop liking him. Don't trust him.*

Kate gave Matt a quick hug, which he gladly accepted. "So I was supposed to take Brenna out for a ride today to show her around the ranch trails, but I've been... um, unexpectedly called away. I don't suppose you were planning on going out for a ride and could maybe take her with you?"

Brenna's cheeks started to burn as she stood there waiting to see what he said when Kate asked him. Honestly, what was wrong with her? Matt wouldn't hurt her, especially here on the ranch for all to see. She needed to learn to look passed the fear her father had instilled in her. *Most people aren't waiting for the opportunity to hurt you,* she reminded herself.

"Well, I hadn't really thought about it, but if it means I get the chance to spend the afternoon with a pretty girl, I'm not going to say no. Lucky for you, I brought my good hat to wear." He winked at her as he pulled out a wool hat to put on. "I used to be as bald as a cue ball, so I still always keep a warm hat nearby for emergencies."

Brenna couldn't help but laugh. "Why were you bald? Don't men usually have hair then go bald, not the other way around?" She tried to picture him without his golden red hair, but it was impossible to do so.

Matt shrugged and cast his eyes away before quickly looking back to Brenna and Kate. "Let's just say in my previous job, someone with red hair wouldn't have been taken very seriously."

She could definitely tell he was keeping something to himself, but she couldn't figure out what kind of job would discriminate against a redhead. Especially here in Anchorage where the people all seemed so nice.

She decided not to press for more information. Everyone had their own secrets to carry. Besides, the last thing she needed was for them to get close, or for him to think it would be okay to start digging into her past. Despite the push and pull of her emotions, she needed to be a little brave and take a step forward in her recovery.

"If you're okay with it," she told him after swallowing back her hesitation, "I'd love to go riding with you." All Brenna could think about was getting on the back of Buddy and riding until all of her troubles were far behind her. If Matt was the key to making that happen today, then she'd suck it up and trust him.

Just for today.

Just this once.

CHAPTER 7

BRENNA SAT HIGH AND TALL IN THE SADDLE AS A GENTLE wind blew past her. She and Matt were barely moving at more than a slow walk, but that didn't lessen her excitement one bit.

And then Matt said, "I think we're going to see our first snowfall today. Look at the mountains." He pointed off in the distance. "See how the snowcaps have almost worked their way down the mountain? It's a bit early in the season, but no denying the facts."

Brenna thought she could have died of happiness right then and there. A fresh blanket of white to cover up all the ugliness of the past would be just the ticket. Excitedly, she glanced around in search of the fat flakes she so hoped to see, but none had made their way down to earth just yet.

Soon, she thought with a smile. Despite the as-of-yet

absent snow, the air had grown frigid, sending a chill straight through her whenever it found an exposed bit of skin to brush against. That didn't matter, though. Nothing mattered now that she was riding again.

Sitting on top of Buddy as they stepped their way down the trails brought back so many pleasant memories that had once been long forgotten. Why was it that the happy memories faded away so quickly while the awful ones stayed and stayed? For the briefest of times in her life, riding had an escape, a joy, a safe place—and now she had it back.

As soon as they'd started out from the ranch, her body grew heavy with relaxation for the first time in so long she had almost forgot how it felt to simply let go and lose herself to the moment.

Matt was a good guide, mostly leaving her to her thoughts as she took in the wonders that spread in every direction around her. Sitting astride his horse in full winter regalia made him look even more prince-like than he had before. Brenna let herself pretend she was part of a royal cavalcade—or maybe even the princess herself.

As she was taking in the site of a frozen over stream at the bottom of a deep valley, a fat little flake drifted across the scene—first one, then a dozen more as if the sky itself had opened up and decided to dance its way to earth.

Brenna gasped with delight.

"Everything all right?" Matt asked with a smirk as their horses slowed even further.

"Everything is perfect," she answered, not caring that it may be an overreaction. This was special to her, and if Matt decided to judge her for it, then it would be easier to push him aside and keep her distance.

Matt stared at her for a moment before glancing up toward the sky. "It's really starting to come down now. Since it's still a bit warm out for snow, it's going to be a wet and heavy snowfall. The perfect kind for building a snowman." He grinned over at her like a little boy who was excited for his chance to play outside in the snow.

"Should we head back to the ranch?" Brenna was so happy to see the snow, but she also wasn't sure if it was safe to be out in it like this. What if it turned into a blizzard? What if they got stranded?

He laughed softly and shook his head, then turned his horse down a new trail. "No, there's no need to turn back, unless you're afraid of turning into a giant frozen popsicle. Florida, right?"

"Yes, *Florida*. That's why I have no idea what to expect from all this snow. We won't actually freeze. Will we?" She laughed aloud when he stopped and turned to look at her again in surprise. She enjoyed being able to relax and joke around with someone like this—even if she was still unsettled by the fact that it was with a man. And a handsome one at that.

"All this snow?" he quipped. "Darling, you ain't seen nothing yet."

They continued along the trail side by side, quietly enjoying the ride while the snow began to fall heavier around them. Brenna couldn't stop smiling. It was like a giant snow globe come to life and she was right in the center of it all.

She lifted her face to the sky to let the flakes land on her cheeks, then stuck her tongue out to catch one. It tasted light and perhaps a little sweet, and she absolutely loved it. After catching another on the tip of her tongue, she spotted Matt staring at her with a besotted grin.

Brenna's cheeks burned with embarrassment at being caught doing something so childish. "Sorry, I've just never had the chance to do that before. I've seen people do it in the movies and always thought it was a bit silly, but when I was out here in the snow I just had this urge and—"

"You talk a lot. Do you know that?" Matt looked up and stuck his own tongue out. When he caught one, he looked back at her and grinned. "You never need to apologize for enjoying the simple things in life. And I haven't done that since I was a kid. Did it taste like ice cream to you?"

"Yes," she exclaimed. "How it that even possible?"

"I guess we taste what we want it to be. Mine was butter pecan. What was yours?"

"Mmm, mint chocolate chip. My favorite."

They laughed together taking turns to catch ice cream flavored snowflakes on their tongues as they continued down the trail. The path narrowed and Matt pulled ahead to lead the way. Brenna watched his back as he poked along the trail in front of her. His shoulders were wide beneath his thick coat, and the wool hat on his head only left a few pieces of his reddish hair exposed around the rim. He looked comfortable in a saddle even if he was, in fact, the farthest thing from a cowboy she could imagine.

She thought back to the day she'd gotten her tattoo and remembered that both of his arms had been fully covered in ink, though she couldn't recall any of the specific artwork he sported. Still, he'd looked more like a gangster than a man who'd enjoy a quiet ride on the back of a horse.

She guessed it was true you couldn't judge a book by its cover.

Brenna caught up to him and rode beside him as they came into an open spot on the trail. "Did you grow up nearby?" she wondered aloud.

He looked off into the distance toward the mountain peaks that were looming over the trees. "I've lived in Anchorage all my life. I can't imagine being anywhere else than here in Alaska. I know some people hate the cold winters, but I love the snow. It's all I've ever known, I guess." His eyes moved to her face. "How about you? Were you always in Florida until recently?"

Her chest tightened at the talk of her own past life. But she couldn't expect Matt to know she didn't like talking about it. There was also no way he knew about the secret bruises that had long since faded. She sighed despite herself. "I grew up in a small town about a half hour south of Orlando. One of those towns where everyone thinks they know everything about everybody else's business. I hated it there and couldn't get away fast enough once I was able to."

His eyes held hers and his eyebrows pulled together in concern. "Is your family still there?"

Brenna's heart began to gallop. *He doesn't know a single thing. How could he? You're safe. Safe.* She gulped before continuing, "My mom and sister are there. My dad passed away about a year ago."

Matt cleared his throat and cast his eyes toward the ground. "Oh, I'm sorry."

"Don't be. The world isn't any worse off without him in it." As soon as the words came out, she bit her lip to stop anymore from spilling forth. Why did she say that? She normally didn't say a word about her dad. Peeking at Matt, she could see that he was once again watching her intently, but thankfully he didn't push for more. He seemed to sense that it was a subject that she preferred not to discuss.

"How about your family? Are they all still in Anchorage?" she asked, hoping he'd grab tight to the change of topic and run with it.

Matt nodded. The trace of a smile played at his handsome features. "My parents still live here in the same house I grew up in. I have a sister who moved to Oregon a few years ago for a job. We never really had much growing up, so I think she works extra hard to ensure she never has to live in poverty again."

The snow continued to swirl down from the skies around them, but the moment for playfully catching flakes had long since passed.

Matt cleared his throat again. "I never really saw a reason to leave here. I owe it to my parents to stick around and make up for things I did that I'm... not proud of."

Brenna's mind swirled now, too. What could he have possibly done? She knew asking for his past would open up the opportunity to ask about hers, so she stayed quiet despite her curiosity.

Matt caught her gaze and frowned. "Sorry, didn't mean to get all depressing on you there. Most of the people I know like Liz, Dorian, Sofia, and some of the other friends I used to have, they all have these loud, larger than life personalities. Sometimes I feel like I get pushed into the background while they take over. But with you... well, it's like we're just hanging out in the background together, and I like it. That probably came out all wrong, but you just seem so comfortable in your skin, like you don't have anything to prove. It's refreshing, I guess is what I'm trying to say."

Brenna tried—and failed—to stifle a laugh. Her? Comfortable in her skin? No way! Was Matt seeing a part of her that she'd never noticed before, or was he just projecting onto her what he wanted to believe about himself? Either way, it was kind of hilarious.

"Well, I'm glad you find my heartfelt confession amusing," he said with a wink. "Tell you what, —we've been serious enough for the day. Time to go back to having fun. Let's head up to that ridge over there so you can get a good view of the whole ranch. It's going to be beautiful now with this fresh snow lying on the ground around us." He kicked his heels into his horse's sides and rode off before she could answer.

Brenna and Buddy took chase, riding faster than she had in her whole life and loving every moment of it. The only bad part of the whole day is how much she felt her guard lowering around Matt. She'd need to be more careful or she just might end up falling in love despite her better judgment.

CHAPTER 8

BRENNA FOLLOWED MATT TO THE RIDGE, AMAZED AT HOW effortlessly he dismounted and plopped to the ground below. He offered to help her down, but she refused. Her shaky landing brought forth giggles from both of them.

"Laugh at me, will you?" She suddenly had an urge and she smiled to herself as she looked over at Matt, who was staring out at the mountains in the distance. Pulling her arm back, she quickly flung the snowball she'd just made at him. It fell apart as soon as it hit his arm, and she suddenly worried that he might be angry with her.

But when he turned and smiled, raising an eyebrow in surprise, she had to laugh. "Did you seriously just throw a snowball at me?" he asked, racing over to her side.

She shrugged innocently. "Well, you've been so understanding about all these new firsts for me, so I thought *maybe* you'd appreciate the fact that I'd never actually had a chance to throw a snowball at anyone before. And just maybe you'd also like being my first."

He rolled his eyes and laughed as he shook his head and bounded over to check on the horses. "Glad I could help you make that happen."

Brenna bent down and picked up a second handful of wet snow and made it into a ball. They'd been out now for a couple of hours and her cheeks were chilled, but she was enjoying every moment. The snow had continued to fall and now, as they stood on the top of the hill overlooking the ranch, she was contemplating the white stuff that had accumulated on the ground. "I always thought this stuff would be a lot fluffier," she admitted as she packed even more snow onto her quickly growing projectile.

He finished what he was doing then turned to face her, leaning slightly against his horse. "The snow is normally fluffy during the colder winter, but since it's still a bit warm outside, the first few snowfalls can be a lot heavier and stickier. This is the best snow for making snowballs to hurl at people. Or for building that snowman I was talking about before. Maybe we should let you cross that off your bucket list, too. This is the perfect place for one overlooking the ranch below."

"Are you serious? We have time?" Brenna dropped her snowball in surprise, then quickly straightened and tried to play it casual. She was a grown woman, after all, who shouldn't be getting this excited over something like this. Still, she couldn't suppress the grin that spread across her face.

Matt laughed and came over to join her, then bent down to make a snowball of his own. "You have to do it like this. Make a big mound of snow, then start rolling it over the snow to pick up more. Keep working it into a ball shape as you go. I'll do the big one for the bottom if you do the middle ball."

Brenna watched him for a moment, then bent down and mimicked his actions. It turned out the process was actually quite a bit harder than it looked as she struggled to keep the ball from falling apart as it grew in size. Also, snow got heavy fast!

Matt finished his, then came over to help her. He leaned over beside her and helped her push it, their hands bumping into each other as they worked together. He glanced her way and smiled, but kept pushing the ball forward until they rolled it up to his. "As you can see, it's a bit heavy, so I'll lift it onto the base while you, my pretty, start making the smaller one for his head."

She tittered at the ridiculous nickname. He sounded just like the Wicked Witch of the West. Her heart raced faster, and Brenna wasn't entirely sure if it was from working so hard to make the snowball or if it was from

Matt's nearness and his compliments. It wasn't like she'd actually touched his hand when they bumped each other. They were both wearing big gloves. But she was sure she'd still felt a sudden jolt of something between them. She'd been called pretty before, too, but it never made her heart swell. Not like this.

She shook her head and rolled her eyes at herself. She was being ridiculous.

Moving on!

Brenna distracted herself by getting down in the snow again and setting to work on the snowball for their man's head. She focused on the feel of the cold that surrounded her and willed her mind to be as blank as the fat, fluffy flakes that continued to fall from the sky. Matt was a nice guy who'd offered to take her for a ride, and she was a broken woman who was on the ranch to get help. That's just how things were going to be. She needed to keep her heart and her body under control, end of story.

"That's pretty much perfect, just like that." Matt came over and hefted the ball into his arms, walking the short distance to their snowman and dropping this third and final mound on top.

"Now you need to put some snow between the balls to keep it secure. That's how all the best snowmen are made." He picked up some snow and showed her how to press it in between the creases to secure the newly erected structure.

Her eyes kept wandering to him, watching him as he worked so intently on making this perfect snowman with her.

"So now what will we use for his eyes?" He crouched down and dug in the snow until he found some stones on the trail. He held his hand out for her to take them. "This is your snowman, Brenna, so you should have the honor of giving him his sight."

They worked together, sticking two broken branches into the sides for arms and using some other rocks to make a mouth and some buttons.

"He'll be cold. Don't snowmen usually need a scarf or something? All the ones I've seen, you know, on TV and in the movies have one." Brenna laughed as he brought his hand up to rub his chin and pretend to think about it seriously.

Finally, Matt pulled his own out from under his jacket. "Well, I don't want your first snowman to be anything less than perfect, so I guess he can have my good scarf. Luckily I'm tough and can handle a bit of cold while we ride back to the ranch." He handed it to her with a wide grin.

"Are you sure? It looks like a pretty nice scarf." She walked up to the snowman and waited until he nodded before tying it around the neck.

When it was all done, she came over and stood beside him to admire their work. "He's perfect! That scarf was just what he needed. Thank you so much for this day, Matt. It's just what *I* needed." She lifted her head to smile up at him and caught her breath when her eyes met his.

He didn't say anything but slowly turned to face her, locking his eyes on hers. That was when Brenna noticed they were sparkling with some untold mirth.

Should I tell him I'm not looking for a relationship, or is that too presumptuous? Is he going to kiss me? No, why would he want to do a thing like that? But then, why is he looking at me like that? Oh my gosh, what do I do next? Brenna's internal monologue ran through her head so quickly she could hardly catch on to a single thought, and when Matt reached forward to grab her hands in his, she froze.

"No, thank you, Brenna," he said as Brenna's heart thumped in her ears. "Seeing someone have the chance to do all of this for the first time and being able to enjoy it all through your eyes has been amazing."

Before she had time to make any further sense of what was happening, Matt's face lowered and his lips found hers. Brenna's pulse raced as he gently pulled her closer to him, bringing his arm around her back. Her own arms went up to hold onto the front of his jacket as she struggled to keep her knees from buckling under her. She'd been kissed before, but never like this. There was so much promise in Matt's kiss that, for the briefest of moments, she allowed herself to believe there were men out there who could be trusted.

But half a second later, reality hit her straight in the chest.

No, they couldn't. Men would always be stronger and able to hurt a woman at their whim. She refused to be a victim ever again. She couldn't allow herself to lose focus. She couldn't compromise her recovery due to a couple enjoyable afternoons in Matt's presence.

Get out of there. Get to safety!

Brenna pushed hard against Matt's chest and leaped back, bringing her hands to her mouth to stifle the scream she felt building within her.

Matt turned bright red with embarrassment, regret, *something.* "I'm sorry, Brenna. I didn't mean...I mean...I'm sorry. I thought you were feeling the same things as me. I shouldn't have overstepped."

Her heart clenched as she saw the genuine pain in his eyes as he thought he'd done something to hurt her. But she wasn't going to let herself be fooled. Staring at him through wide eyes, she caught the sob that threatened to break from her throat.

"Let's just forget it ever happened, okay? I think it's time we headed back anyway." Her voice shook as much as her legs as she rushed over to mount Buddy. As soon as she was in the saddle, she kicked in her heels and let him take her home.

Matt kept his distance as he followed behind. Luckily,

Buddy knew the way back to the stables and was more than happy to lead the way.

Brenna felt so confused as she flew across the snowy landscape. For a moment when Matt had kissed her, it felt warm and cozy. It felt like the way things should be. But then the fear of repeating past mistakes slammed into her, coming in waves as the tears rolled down her cheeks.

Why couldn't she just be happy? Didn't she deserve that much after all she'd been through? Could she ever really be free, or would she always be afraid of whatever possibilities life threw her way?

She suspected she knew, and the answer broke her heart.

CHAPTER 9

FOR THE FIRST TIME SINCE HER ARRIVAL AT MEMORY RANCH, Brenna had difficulty sleeping through the night. After waking up for the third time in the space of just a couple hours, she reached for the book she'd borrowed from Liz's personal library and started reading. And by the time the sun came up, she'd finished the entire journey from Anchorage to Nome alongside the author and her spirited team of sled dogs.

Reading Scarlett Cole's great adventures made Brenna's life feel very small by comparison. At least she'd managed to pass the time without replaying the events of her ride with Matt over and over again until they made her sick. She moved through the rest of that day like a zombie, thankful for the numbness her sleep deprivation had brought up.

Fearful of the very real possibility that she might start a

grease fire, she instead chopped meat, vegetables, and potatoes and dumped them into the slow cooker for a hearty yet safe meal to feed the residents. She had to learn new ways to cook in the smaller kitchen and without all of the fancy utensils and appliances she'd learned with in the more industrial restaurant kitchens of her past. Ordinarily, on her more well rested days, using the large crock pot to have meals cooking throughout the day was a good way for her to free up more time for baking while still making sure the evening meal was done on time.

When it came right down to it, being in the kitchen made her happy—and she wouldn't trade that for the world. Cooking and baking were two things she loved, and she could lose herself for hours with just a mixing bowl and spoon to keep her company.

Learning to cook had become vital to her well-being at an inappropriately young age. Her mother was often too hurt to tend to meal preparation, but that didn't change the fact that her father expected a piping hot dinner on the table every night by five o'clock. If they failed at that, there was always a special kind of hell to pay. What else could she do? What else could any of them do?

Brenna had stepped in to make sure the monster was fed and at least couldn't use *that* as an excuse to beat them. For the first few years of this arrangement, she'd needed to use a stool to reach the counter and stovetops. That's how tiny she'd been. Still, he'd complain and catapult the steaming hot food into her face. Sometimes he'd be so dissatisfied in the fruits of her labor that he'd beat her, but at least it meant he wasn't hurting her mother. Those nights off from the abuse had become so important to her mom's well-being that it didn't matter if Brenna had to hurt, too.

With time, practice, and determination, Brenna was able to turn out meals that satisfied both her father's stomach and his temper. Things got better for a little while then, too.

Until suddenly they weren't.

The other shoe always dropped. That had become a fact of life as far as Brenna was concerned, and it's why she had to be so careful still even though her father was gone.

She tried not to think about it as she continued peeling and slicing vegetables for her stew. So what if she'd discovered cooking under duress? It brought her protection then, and it gave her comfort now. Besides, there were far worse ways to spend an afternoon than in a warm, yummy-smelling kitchen.

She finished up with the vegetables and moved on to mix a fresh batch of muffins. That was when she could feel that she was no longer alone. Sure enough, Liz spoke a second later as she hurried through the kitchen toward Brenna.

"Hey, girl, I was hoping I'd catch you in here. How's everything going?" Liz walked into the kitchen and sat down on a stool across the island from where Brenna was working.

She continued mixing the batter she was working on, unable to meet Liz's eyes. Brenna knew she'd been in a bit of a mood since Sunday when she'd been riding with Matt, and she was embarrassed that she'd let others see it.

When she'd raced back to the ranch and dismounted, she'd quickly handed the reins to Howard saying she wasn't feeling well and asked him to take care of Buddy for her. Matt had caught up with her along the way, but he gave Brenna the space she needed without forcing her to talk. As she turned on heel toward her cabin, she heard him telling Howard that he'd brush Buddy down and put him away.

The day after her big kerfuffle with Matt, Liz stopped by to let her know there was an opening with the therapist who specialized in relationship counseling and that Brenna could begin to see her in addition to her regular recovery therapist if she was open to it. Brenna accepted the opening but then pushed Liz out of her cabin before the other woman had a chance to settle in for a more social visit.

Rude or not, Brenna just couldn't talk what had happened with Matt. Not yet. Sometimes she just couldn't seem to get her emotions under control, and she always felt embarrassed after. It also made her worry that she was taking after her father despite her best efforts to be nothing like him.

Like she did now, standing with Liz in the kitchen as if nothing had gone wrong.

"Everything's fine," she lied. "Thanks for setting up that extra session for me. I think it helped." That was a lie, too, because while she found it easy to open up to her normal therapist, this new relationship counselor pushed too hard.

"You can keep seeing her if you want. We were all really worried about you after your ride with Matt on Sunday."

Brenna whipped her head up to look at Liz. "Why?" Had Matt said something, or did Brenna just wear her heart on her sleeve for all to see?

Liz smiled knowingly and shrugged. "Matt told me he might have stepped over a line with you. He feels terrible."

Brenna looked back down at her batter and sighed. "No, he didn't really do anything wrong. I just reacted badly." Her cheeks started to burn as she looked back across at Liz. "He kissed me and I pushed him away, then ran off like I'd been attacked. I didn't mean to do it, but I guess I'm just not ready to let myself believe all men aren't the same."

Liz fixed Brenna with a sorrowful expression. "Matt wouldn't give the details, but I figured it was something like that. Just know that he's had his own share of bad luck in his life and would never want to do anything to intentionally hurt anyone. I'm sure if you talked to him, he'd understand."

"I doubt he'd want to talk to me again after how I acted. I'm a mess, and I'm not sure if that's ever going to change.

You know the worst part? Everything about that afternoon with him up until that point had been pretty much perfect."

"I don't think I've ever heard perfect and Matt used in the same sentence," Liz said with a laugh, but then sobered again after taking in Brenna's dour expression.

Liz put one hand on the counter as she regarded Brenna. "Matt is far from perfect, and I'm sure he'd be the first one to tell you that if you let him. And this might not be easy to hear, but it has to be said..."

Brenna gulped. Here it was, time for the other shoe to drop—and she'd really begun to enjoy her time here.

Liz took a deep breath before continuing. "Until you give him a chance to prove that he isn't like your father, I don't think it's fair to just assume he is."

Brenna stared at her batter, wishing she could just be like everyone else and let herself have a relationship with someone without worrying. She'd had a few relationships in high school and one after that hadn't ended well. And she knew it was all her fault. Her fear always took over.

But Liz was right. She hadn't broached the topic with her before, but Brenna knew that Liz and the staff had a full run-down of her situation when reading over her application and medical referral to the ranch. Still, she felt exposed. It was hard knowing that others already knew the worst things about her, that maybe they expected her to stumble and fall.

Like she had with Matt.

Brenna realized it wasn't fair to assume that he would hurt her the way that her father had, but that didn't make choosing to trust him any easier.

She did like Matt. She did!

And she knew she'd only actually spent a few hours over the span of a couple afternoons in his company, but he didn't *seem* anything like her father at all. And when he'd kissed her she'd had a few seconds of feeling like everything was right in the world. Of course, her fears had pushed their way through and ruined what could have been a blissful moment for her, but the beginnings had been there.

Maybe if she just talked to Matt and tried to explain, he would be patient with her. Liz said he had a troubled past of his own. Did that mean he might understand Brenna's?

And would he even want to talk to her now after how she'd run off like that? What if he thought she was a complete lunatic now? What if her over-the-top reaction had quashed any feelings he'd begun to have for her? What if, what if, what if…?

CHAPTER 10

BRENNA SPENT THE NEXT FEW WEEKS GOING BACK AND FORTH on whether she owed Matt an apology about her role in their disastrous kiss, whether it was safe to see him again, to make even becoming friends official. Her new relationship therapist had helped her see how flawed her thinking was, but that didn't mean she could just undo years of trauma in just a few sessions.

Still, she'd decided to take a chance and bet on Matt, bet on herself.

She stared out the window at the rundown house across the street from where her car idled at the curb. This was the address the man at the tattoo shop had given her, but she still wasn't sure if it was right. When she'd stopped off at Pipeline Ink to apologize to Matt, the artist on staff had explained that Matt had taken the day off to spend some time helping his parents following his mother's surgery. Brenna had typed the address into her phone, not sure if she'd be brave enough to drive over.

And yet here she was.

Staking out Matt's parents' house like some kind of stalker, trying to work up the courage to head to the front door and knock.

What are you doing here? This is crazy! He doesn't want to see you, and you don't owe him any kind of apology. Just put the whole thing behind you and move on!

Brenna took a series of deep breaths. Her inner critic was right. This was one of her worst ideas yet. But just as she was about to start her car back up, drive home, and abandon the whole apologizing idea, the side door swung open revealing Matt carrying a garbage bag and wearing only a pair of plaid pajama pants and slippers.

Brenna's cheeks burned as she tried to crouch down in her seat before he could see her. But it was too late.

He stopped and glanced directly at her. Even from the distance that separated them, she could see his eyebrows pull together in confusion. Slowly, he walked across the street to her car.

She opened the door and stepped out, acting like it was perfectly normal for her to be here. She tried not to notice his well-muscled arms or the tattoos on his chest that she hadn't seen previously. He had a bird in flight just like she did. Why hadn't he mentioned that before? And what did it represent? Okay, now she was staring.

If Matt noticed, he didn't seem to mind. "Brenna? What are you doing here?" He brought his hands up and rubbed furiously at his arms in a futile attempt to keep warm. His skin had already started to take on a faint bluish tinge. What was he doing in this bitter cold without a shirt? He had to be even crazier than she'd thought before.

"Are you okay?" Brenna couldn't help but ask. "You are literally freezing over right before my eyes."

Matt let out a puff of air and rolled his eyes. "Nah, I'm a born and raised Alaskan. I can handle a little cold air. What's up?"

Brenna felt the need to hurry through her explanation and her apology. She'd hate it if Matt died from hypothermia on her account. "Well, I stopped by the shop to talk to you earlier and your friend said you were here. I probably shouldn't have come over unannounced. I mean, the guy mentioned something about your mom having surgery and you being here to help out. Now I feel ridiculous. I shouldn't have come over at all. I'm sorry."

Now she was babbling like a school girl. If he hadn't thought her crazy before, he definitely did now. It wasn't the apology she had envisioned, but it would just have to do. Was it too late to get back in her car and hightail it out of there?

Matt smiled and then laughed. With each chuckle, more and more puffs of air rose form his lungs into the sky. "Brenna, slow down. It's fine. I'm glad you came by. And yes, my mom just had a mastectomy. She's doing well but taking it hard emotionally."

Now she truly did feel like a complete heel. She'd been awful to Matt and here he was going through huge things of his own. Still, he hadn't turned away and he hadn't asked her to leave. Was it true that he still enjoyed seeing her despite... well, everything?

"I'm sorry," she mumbled. "I'll pray for her, if that helps."

"Thanks for that. We'll know in a few weeks if she'll need any more treatment." He rubbed his arms faster trying to get warm. "But I'm sure you really didn't come all this way to talk about my mom."

She swallowed and tried to calm her racing heart. "No, I just wanted to apologize for the other day. I overreacted to... well, you know, and I just wanted to let you know I'm sorry."

Matt nodded and glanced back toward the house. "Do you mind if I go grab a jacket? We could go for a walk and talk a bit. I owe you an apology, too, but I'd like to do it without having to stand here jumping up and down to keep my blood circulating." The smile he gave her caused her breath to catch in her chest.

"Of course. I'll just wait here." She decided not to

mention the fact he'd just said that native born Alaskans could handle the cold without any issue.

"Now why would you do that? Come in and meet my parents. Besides, my mom would have my hide if I left a woman standing out here in the cold waiting for me." His teeth chattered, but he offered her a chivalrous smile nonetheless.

Brenna cringed at the thought of entering Matt's parents' home. That was way too intimate an invitation. "I better not," she hedged. "I mean, if she just got out of surgery, I'm sure she doesn't want some stranger walking into her house."

Matt just laughed and turned to go back across the street, grabbing her hand to pull her behind him. "Trust me. She would be more horrified if I didn't bring you inside. I'll just be a second."

She had no choice but to follow as he led her up the steps and opened the door. She hoped he could grab his sweater and jacket quickly before anyone even noticed she was there.

Unfortunately, they walked straight into the living room where both parents were resting together. His mother lay propped up against a heap of pillows on the couch while Matt's father kept vigil from a well-worn plaid armchair.

Matt jumped straight into introductions. "Hey Mom, I found a friend outside and we're going to go for a walk. I have to get a sweater or something first, though." He pulled

Brenna out from where she was discreetly trying to hide behind him and led her to the edge of the coffee table.

"This is Brenna Barry. She's the new cook out at Memory Ranch." He turned and smiled at her. "And Brenna, this is my mom, Cynthia. And this is my dad, Michael."

"It's very nice to meet you, Brenna," his mom said with a hoarse voice. "I'm glad Matt didn't just leave you standing in the street. His manners aren't usually the best despite how hard we both worked to raise him right."

"Too true, too true." His father bobbed his head in agreement.

Matt returned a moment later, pulling a heavy coat over his shoulders while shaking his head. "Really, Mom? I heard all that, and—no—I'm not that bad. You make me sound like some kind of Neanderthal."

Brenna laughed awkwardly as Matt bent to kiss his mother on the cheek. "It's nice to meet you both. I'm sorry to intrude. I was really just stopping to talk to Matt for a quick second. I didn't realize you'd just got home from the hospital or I wouldn't have bothered you."

His mom just waved her hand in the air. "It's fine. I already like you much better than the crowd Matt usually runs with."

"And that's enough out of you," Matt said, plopping onto the couch to pull big, fuzzy socks over his feet followed by huge, clomping boots.

Brenna stood nervously beside Matt, wishing she could help him dress so it would go faster. The house was cozy inside filled with pictures and mementos that obviously meant a lot to the people who lived inside the walls. The furniture wasn't high end and looked like it was all as old, if not older, than Matt. But it all looked comfortable. Exactly how she'd always pictured a real home would look.

Finally, Matt announced that he was ready and opened the door for Brenna to go out ahead of him. She pulled her scarf up higher and zipped her jacket to the top as a cold wall of air slammed into her. They went down the steps and started walking, the snow beneath their boots crunching with every step.

Okay, it's time to explain why you came. It's not like it can be any more embarrassing than whatever that was, she told herself. She wasn't used to telling her story except to therapists and doctors, but Matt seemed like a good enough person to start with.

Just so long as she didn't lose her nerve.

CHAPTER 11

Brenna kept her arms hugged tight around her waist as she and Matt walked through his neighborhood. The houses were rundown and most of the cars seemed to be nearly as old as her. They passed a woman shoveling her driveway as a pair of toddlers pranced through the snow on either side of her. Brenna smiled, and Matt waved and said hello.

It definitely illustrated that one never knew what was going on behind closed doors. She was proof enough of that, growing up in her nice house with a respected businessman as her father. The inside was far uglier than the outside, whereas Matt's neighborhood seemed like it might be the exact opposite.

They walked past another few houses and then Matt turned to her and said, "I'm so glad you came to talk, Brenna.

I've been wanting to stop by and see you, but I didn't want to overstep and or push you anymore than I did with the... with that day. Honestly, I felt terrible thinking I'd hurt you, but I also didn't know how to make it right without risking the chance I could just make things worse."

He stuffed his hands into his pockets and fixed his eyes back on the horizon as they continued walking side by side. "I'm not usually drawn to people like I am to you. Normally I feel like everyone is trying to show off, but with you, it's like you're trying to sink into the background. It makes me want to know you. That's stupid and I'm probably way off base, but it doesn't change the fact that I really, really like you, Brenna. It's okay if you don't feel the same way. I mean, why would you want a guy like me with my sordid past and pushy kisses?"

Brenna stopped walking suddenly and turned to face him on the sidewalk as a car slowly drove through the snowy street. She couldn't have him accepting the blame for that day, especially for reasons that had nothing to do with anything. She'd probably sent *kiss me* signals left and right. She was always making mistakes like that—and she'd wanted that kiss every bit as much as she hadn't wanted it.

"Matt, I don't think you're the one who needs to apologize," she said, keeping her arms hugged tightly around herself for an added layer of support and protection. "And my reaction had nothing at all to do with the kind of guy you think you are. I don't know anything about your past that would allow me to judge you one way or another. Besides, it's not like I have the picture perfect past myself."

He crinkled his eyebrows together and tipped his head to the side. "You mean Liz never mentioned anything to you? About my history? I assumed you knew and that's why you ran away from me like that. She never told me about why you came to the ranch, by the way. She keeps all her residents' info private, but I'm not a resident, so…"

What was he talking about? There was nothing she knew about him that could possibly be as bad as her own story.

Matt turned and slowly started walking again, so she moved to keep up. She stared at him dumbfounded and shook her head. "I ran away because of *me*, not because of you. I'm damaged goods, Matt."

"Now, see, I don't believe that for a second. I really like everything I've seen about you so far."

She refused to believe that. If she was good, then this would be much easier. Instead, she was a hot mess. The sooner Matt figured that out, the better. "Even my running away?"

Matt shrugged. "There's nothing wrong with taking your time to decide about things. More people should do it. *I* should've done it."

"Matt, it's not your fault. I... I was abused. By my father," she admitted shyly.

"I was hoping it wouldn't be something like that. You never know with the ranch, and I didn't want to pry, but..." A strange mix of emotions crossed Matt's face before he asked, "Did he ever...?"

Brenna knew exactly what he was trying to ask. It was the same thing everyone got around to asking when they heard about her history, whether it was any of their business or not. "Gosh, no!" she shouted. "He hit me, pushed me, beat me, but never, *never* touched me. Not like that."

Relief flashed across his face followed by a deep frown. "I'm sorry for what you went through. I have no idea what that's like, but I know you didn't deserve it. My mistakes... well, they were of my own making."

Brenna kept her eyes on the ground before them. It was easier that way.

"I've done things I'm not proud of and if I could go back and do my life differently, I would," he said, stopping then to let out a deep sigh. "I won't go too much into the why, because it's the what that matters in the end. Right?"

Brenna let him talk, knowing somehow that he just had to get it all in the open. She could understand that, even if she wasn't quite ready to talk about the specifics of her own past.

He stopped and turned to face her again, waiting for her

to return his gaze before he continued. "I was a junkie and a dealer for a while, too. That's just who I thought I was meant to be so I wouldn't end up some poor sap who struggled paycheck to paycheck for the rest of my life. My friends then—and clients—they made me feel like I was important. They were always so happy to see me, and I guess I let it get to my head.

"I didn't realize that they didn't actually care about me—only what I had to offer them. And that made it so hard to see that I needed a change. See, that's why it means so much to me that you're just... real. Few people are these days. By the way, I finally did change. That was a couple years back. I had another friend who found a way out—Sofia. She helped me do the same, and I haven't looked back for a single second since."

Brenna's heart pounded heavy in her chest. She couldn't even focus on the compliment he'd given her, not with all he'd revealed. He was an addict? Like her father? But that meant...

Oh, no.

"Don't look so worried." Matt's laugh caught her off guard. "It's not like I killed anyone."

Despite his laugh, she could see the shame in Matt's eyes as he discussed his past. She hated that, for even a brief moment, she wondered if she could ever give someone like him a chance knowing his less than savory history. After all, growing up with a father like she'd had, Brenna knew how hard it was for people to change—especially addicts.

What if Matt's past came calling? What if, deep down, he still craved that importance, that high? Falling for Matt was even riskier than she'd originally imagined.

It all made perfect sense. She had every reason to stay away now that he'd confided his secret in her. And yet her heart didn't want to let go. Not yet...

"Well, I appreciate your honesty with me," she said, knowing he was waiting for a response. "You didn't have to tell me, but I'm glad you did. I understand you much better now, but I still have so many issues of my own, issues I need to work through. It's why I'm here. At the ranch, I mean." She swallowed and looked past Matt's shoulder to watch a cat walk up the sidewalk across the street. It hopped onto a railing and made its way up to a house where it perched on the front step, waiting to be noticed. It was easier to watch the cat than look into his eyes.

"You see, where you talk about growing up in a home without any money but filled with love, my story is the complete opposite." She swallowed hard, debating how much she should share now—or ever. *It doesn't hurt for him to know the basics. In fact, it might help.*

"My dad was a big business guy who drank every day and spent every night at home beating his family behind closed doors," she continued stonily, trying to distance herself from the memories as best she could. "To the outside world, we were the perfect family with money, prestige, and the big beautiful house. But inside we spent our time cowering in fear, wondering if we'd survive until the next day."

She was finally able to look at him, scared of what she'd see. She couldn't stand to see the pity or disbelief like she'd seen on so many faces over the years.

But Matt wasn't showing any of those emotions—he just looked angry. "I hate that he hurt you, Brenna. And your mom, too?" His voice shook with fury.

"He did. I have a younger sister, too, but the two of us took most of the brunt of it for her. She's not very strong and I don't think she could have survived it, so I always made sure when he was about to turn on her that I'd get him focused back on me. I tried to convince my mom to leave him so we could all just get away, but he had complete control of everything. He'd completely alienated my mom from her own family and friends. She had no job or money of her own, and he knew it. She had no one to turn to, nowhere to go."

Brenna blinked back tears and fixed her eyes on the ground. "At least that's how I understand it now. How I'm trying to reconcile the fact she didn't save us. For years I was just *so angry* with her. I blamed her. But now..." She shrugged like it didn't matter, even though it mattered more than anything. "I'm realizing just how scared she was and that, at the time, she didn't feel like she had any way out."

Lifting her gaze to his, she fought the tears that were trying to fall. "And I don't ever want to be in that position again. So, Matt, that's why I ran from you that day. I ran away as fast as I could because I'm far too broken to ever be able to trust any man ever again. I'm sorry if that's not what you wanted to hear, but it's the truth. *My* truth."

CHAPTER 12

ANOTHER CAR DROVE PAST THEM, TIRES CRUNCHING through the snow on the street. Brenna kept her eyes on the vehicle, hoping Matt would be the one to say something to break the silence that had enveloped them. She'd never meant to tell him so much or share the feelings she'd carried with her for years. Those were words she'd only ever spoken to the therapist at the ranch. Maybe having already said them once had opened the floodgates. Or maybe, deep down, she desperately wanted this man to understand, hoped that he wouldn't give up on her.

She'd never felt that before in her life.

Matt hesitated before placing a gentle hand on her shoulder. His eyes were filled with kindness... and something else she couldn't quite identify. "Brenna, you're not broken. What your father did to you is unforgivable, and the fact that you're even standing here right now shows us both how strong—*how unbreakable*—you are. Please..."

He let out a deep sigh and chanced a smile. "Look, I know your dad is why you have trouble getting close to people. And I could ask you to trust me and tell you I'm different, but those would just be words. So how about we spend time together until you decide for yourself whether I'm worth taking the chance on. I already know it'll be worth it for me."

Brenna breathed in and out slowly as she tried to force her racing heart to slow down. She wanted to believe in him, to believe in herself, too. She wanted to really try to move past her issues, to maybe even forge a real relationship with Matt. The fear she'd held onto her whole life, however, kept whispering in her ear, saying that he was only telling her what she wanted to hear.

Her dad had been a pro at bending the truth, of only showing people what he wanted them to see. He'd told so many lies to family, friends, and colleagues about his life at home that Brenna was sure he'd almost started to believe them himself. If his wife had a black eye for any kind of black-tie event, it was always easily explained by a fall or some other kind of accident. And since she never said otherwise, their perfect-picture life was believed—or at least not challenged—by everyone who knew them.

He was downright jovial, cracking jokes and telling

stories to his friends. He had a silver tongue, and most were willing to overlook inconsistencies in his lies. But still... why didn't anyone ever dig deeper? Why had no one seen past the cheery façade and uncovered the ugliness beneath?

Matt's soft voice wedged between her thoughts. "You're free from it now. It doesn't have to control you." His words were whispered as he held her face firmly between his hands. The words were almost identical to what she'd been told in therapy, but coming from him, they seemed to chip at the shell she'd constructed around herself.

He seemed to understand, but could she trust him?

Not trusting anyone all these years hadn't healed her. Trying to fade into the background had still got her noticed. Maybe it was time to do something crazy. Maybe it was time to trust no matter how much that terrified her.

"Okay," she said at last, her heart thrumming in her chest. "I'd like to try, too. We have nothing to lose, I guess." She didn't want to admit that she could possibly lose her heart, that she could somehow move even further away from recovery, that everything could always get much, much worse even when it seemed like that would be impossible.

Matt's smile grew from cheek to cheek, unable to be contained. "As *unenthusiastic* as that sounds, I'll take it. I could say there's a risk of losing my pride, but I've probably already done that, right?"

He turned and winked at her, and Brenna couldn't help

but smile, too. "We'll start slow and easy—an outing for friends. I promise I won't try to kiss you again until you ask me to. *If* you ask me to. Okay, so tell me this: have you ever been ice skating before?"

Brenna laughed and shook her head. "I grew up in Florida, remember? Ice skating wasn't exactly the state sport."

He clapped his hands together then rubbed them quickly, either for warmth or to indicate that he had a really hot idea. Maybe both.

"It's settled, then," he said like the cat who ate the canary. "I'm taking you ice skating. If you think playing in the snow is fun, just wait until you get a pair of skates on your feet. There's an outdoor skating rink downtown that's only open in the winters. They've been working all week to get it finished for the season, and it opens this weekend. We can go Saturday night after you're done at work. That is, if you want to?"

Brenna bit her lip. They were moving forward again. It all felt so fast.

You need this. You need him.

Still, she hesitated. "I don't know. Won't there be a lot of people there? What if I can't learn? What if I fall down or make a fool of myself?"

"Easy. I'll help you. I'm kind of a pro, you know? I'll have you doing triple axels in no time."

They both laughed at that. Brenna secretly tucked away

the thought of Matt in a sequined ice dancing costume in case she needed cheering up later. The image was too amusing to only visit once.

And, seriously, how could he seem to take her from discussing some of her deepest secrets, to laughing and feeling excited about something in less than a few minutes?

She rolled her eyes playfully and bumped Matt's shoulder with her own. "Well, if I get hurt and can't work next week, I'll expect you to cover for me."

"You really wouldn't want me to do that. Not if you want to keep your job." He grimaced before breaking apart in laughter once more.

They passed a house Brenna recognized—the same one that had sported the mother and her two toddlers earlier. The drive was now clean and everyone had gone inside. Brenna pictured them munching on grilled cheeses and drinking piping hot tomato soup. She'd have to make that classic comfort meal for the residents at the ranch sometime, too.

When they reached his parents' house a few moments later, Matt stopped and turned toward her with a smile of absolute bliss splashed across his handsome face. "Thank you for coming to talk to me, Brenna. And for this walk. And for agreeing to go ice skating. Thank you for all of it. Thank you for everything."

She looked away, feeling terribly awkward in the

moment. "Maybe don't thank me so much until we see where things go."

"I can't wait." Matt squeezed both of her hands before turning and pointing to the house. "Want to come in for a quick drink? My mom will have my hide if I don't at least try to show you that she has, in fact, taught me basic manners. Shocking, I know."

"Maybe next time," Brenna said, offering him a wave goodbye. She watched fondly as Matt jogged back inside to warm up, leaving her alone with her thoughts, her fears, and even the tiny spark of hope.

CHAPTER 13

DESPITE HER DETERMINATION DURING THEIR TALK, IT HAD taken Matt two whole weeks to convince Brenna to finally go ice skating with him. In the meantime, they stuck mostly to walks, grooming the horses at the ranch together, and even built a few additional snowmen. Each afternoon spent in his company put her more at ease, but she still had a hard time letting her guard down.

Especially now that she faced the very real risk of literally falling down and face planting on the thick ice.

"Whatever you do, don't let go of me!" she cried. "Otherwise, I won't just fall onto the ice. Knowing my luck, I'll fall straight through. Then I'll die from the cold and—oops—no more Brenna."

"Wow, I had no idea you were so dramatic," Matt said as

she gripped his arm tighter and tighter. "You'll be fine. I've got you."

She picked up her left foot and moved it forward a millimeter, maybe less, then did the same with her right. "I really don't think I can do this. How do people actually stand on these things?"

Brenna shook her head in amazement as other skaters flew past them, gliding along the ice as though they were standing on nothing but sharp blades holding them upright on the slippery surface. She'd never been the athletic type, and that definitely showed now.

In middle school her gym coach had suggested she try out for the track team since she loved running so much and often finished their relay races first in class, but her father had quickly put an end to that. Other than sneaking out for an occasional run at home, she hadn't had the opportunity to work on fitness—or even more regrettably at this particular moment, coordination.

Matt laughed and pulled her out a bit farther, then turned and faced her, taking both hands in his as he skated backward. "Just get a feel for the skates under you. Don't try moving yet, and definitely don't walk on the ice. *Glide.* I'll pull you along with me, so you can see how it's supposed to feel."

How did she ever let herself get talked into this? She knew she was going to go down at least once before this night was over, and she also knew it was going to hurt. But she had to admit, it was somehow *still* fun, especially with Matt at her side. He didn't seem to mind that he was stuck looking after some ridiculous girl who couldn't even stand up straight at the moment as he dragged her along the ice.

At least a couple dozen other people dotted the ice rink, but Brenna felt as if she and Matt had this moment solely to themselves. He stayed near the edge, so they'd be out of everyone's way, but it was also more than that. As they made their way around the track, she took a moment to just enjoy the feeling of nothing weighing on her. This was her chance to simply enjoy being alive and further get to know this man who was so patiently holding her upright.

So far he hadn't let go, and if that didn't prove she could trust him, nothing would.

Bright orange lights lined the track, giving off a glow that reflected on the snow around them. She could hear children laughing and shouting as they crisscrossed between the other skaters in some kind of impromptu race. A sweet elderly couple skated past holding hands and smiling at each other. She idly wondered if people thought she and Matt were also a sweet couple, if maybe it was starting to be a little bit true.

"You know what?" she told Matt over the gently whipping wind.

"What?" he asked with a warm smile.

"I've decided it's not natural for humans to be trying to move around ice like this on blades of steel. That's why it's so hard—because it's not normal or right." As soon as she started to talk, her left foot scooted out in front again, almost kicking poor Matt in the shins.

She squealed before continuing. "And I actually think this might be dangerous. I'm going to end up cutting you with the blades of these skates when I fall. You do realize that, right?"

Matt just laughed and shook his head. "Stop talking and just concentrate. And if you do start to fall, try aiming your skates away from my body." He was grinning widely at her, his wool hat pulled down over his head and cheeks red from the cold. She could see his breath whenever he spoke. Sometimes she caught glimpses of her own, too, but mostly she was focused on her feet and the thick ice beneath them.

When Brenna had lived in Florida, she'd always dreamed of living somewhere with snow and cold winters. The thought of curling up with hot chocolate in front of a fire seemed like the perfect cozy way to spend an evening after being outside. However, she didn't think the chill she felt deep in her bones right now could ever be eased by a cup of hot cocoa.

"I'm going to let go of your hands. Just move your skates slowly beneath you. Don't try pushing off them too much."

As he said this, he began to pry her fingers from his and let her slowly drift on her own.

"No! Don't let go. I'm not ready to do this on my own. I think I need more lessons." She gripped onto his hands tightly, refusing to let go. Normally, getting and staying close to him for so long would make her nervous, but the thought of doing this without him was absolutely terrifying.

He tilted his head and raised an eyebrow. "C'mon, tough tattooed girl like you afraid of a little pain?" He looked around at the other skaters. "Besides, I think there's a toddler over there who started the same time as you and she's already going along on her own."

Brenna scowled at him in annoyance. Still, he wasn't exactly wrong. If a little kid could master this, perhaps she could, too. "You better be right about that, because if I fall and break something, I'm pretty much never talking to you again," she announced.

Slowly, she unfolded her fingers and let him pull his hands away. Her arms immediately went out to the sides as she struggled to keep her balance. "I'm scared to move my legs. I know as soon as I do I'm going to be picking ice out of my teeth."

Matt's laughter made her smile. Even if she was about to fall and break her neck, she had to admit it was a lot of fun to be able to joke around with someone like this. It felt natural. And besides, she'd already remained upright for much longer than she'd expected to. Maybe Matt was right. Maybe she could do this. Maybe he was right about other things as well.

"Just move them real slow and smooth," he instructed. "You can do it, Brenna. And I promise, I'll catch you if you fall."

Her eyes lifted to his at the sound in his voice as he spoke. She didn't know if he realized what he was saying, but there was something in the words that wrapped around her heart and squeezed tight. He would catch her. He promised, and she sensed that even implied to situations outside of ice skating, too.

She pushed one foot forward, then the other, moving slowly at first, but then a little faster. Not much, but a little. She couldn't help the wide grin that spread across her face as she realized: "I'm doing it! I'm really doing it!"

She brought her hands in to clap in amusement, but—of course—as soon as she did, each of her feet decided to skate in opposite directions. She ended up hunched over, her legs spread wide as she tried to hold herself up and somehow bring her legs back to a standing position. "Matt! Help me!"

He laughed so hard, it took him a moment to compose himself.

Well, Brenna didn't have a moment. She could just make out the tip of his skates as she carefully peeked up to see if he was helping yet. "I'm serious. I feel like Bambi out here."

Finally, his skates moved into her view and she held her

hands up for him to take. As she moved, her balance went off and immediately her right leg slipped, lifting high in the air as she started to fall.

Matt grunted as the blade caught his shin, but just before she landed hard on the ice, his hand grabbed hers and gently guided her to the ground.

Unfortunately, he must have misjudged her weight because as soon as she was on the ground, he toppled down beside her. He was right, though. It hadn't hurt at all.

Afraid she'd hurt *him*, however, she studied his body for signs of breaks or blood. "Matt, I'm so sorry! Is your leg hurt?"

His laugh rung out across the ice and snow—deep, loud, merry. "Nope, the only thing that hurt is my pride. See? Told you I would catch you."

CHAPTER 14

Brenna and Matt left the skating track earlier than they'd originally planned, but the air had grown so deeply cold that neither could stand being outside much longer. It seemed most of the other skaters had the same idea, and soon they found themselves waiting for a long line of cars leading up to a single stoplight.

Brenna's phone buzzed with a text: *Mom says you're not coming home for Christmas?!*

Sorry, Brenna typed back as she tried to push aside the feelings of guilt that immediately took over. She knew it was hard for her younger sister to understand why she had to leave. And Brenna did feel terrible knowing that she'd left Olivia alone with their mother. But she'd do it all over again if given the chance.

For the first time in her life, Brenna had learned to put

herself first. *An empty vessel can't fill,* her therapist had told her. If she kept giving pieces of herself away to everyone else, there wouldn't be anything left. She wanted to fade into the background, yes, but not disappear.

Her phone buzzed again with another message from Olivia. *Well, Christmas is still almost a month away. I'm sure you'll change your mind. Just don't wait too long because flights are crazy expensive this time of year.*

Brenna put her phone back in her pocket and offered Matt an apologetic smile. She hadn't even realized they'd made it through traffic stop and were now in line at a drive thru for one of Anchorage's famous coffee shacks that offered hot beverages guaranteed to kick you in the butt.

"Everything okay?" Matt asked, studying her as he handed her a warm cup of hot chocolate. How had he known she'd been fantasizing about just this thing earlier that night?

She sank back into the seat and took an appreciative sip, savoring the warmth as it spread through her body. Her phone vibrated in her pocket again. "Thanks for the cocoa," she said, raising the cup to him in a salute. "I'm fine. It's just my sister is having a hard time understanding why I *ran away to Alaska*, as she puts it."

"Ugh, it's never easy when family fights." Matt accepted his change from the cashier and pulled back onto the main road before continuing. "She'll come around, though.

Everyone has their own way of dealing with things. With time, she'll understand that for you, getting better meant getting away from the place where all the memories first played out."

Wow, he really gets it.

Brenna smiled as she tipped her head and watched him. How could this man she'd only met already understand better than her own family? Should she tell him the rest and see if he got that, too? Perhaps it would help if he understood why she'd...

No. It was too soon. She didn't want to confront that memory yet, and she also didn't want to lose Matt. Yes, he came from a rough-and-tumble past of his own, but he'd never done anything half as bad as what she'd been through. What she did.

He sat watching the road ahead, completely unaware of the struggle tearing at her insides. When he turned his head, their eyes met briefly before he turned back to pay attention to driving.

Her insides melted, and she knew it wasn't from the hot chocolate. It was that smile. It was picturing him bald or in an ice-dancing costume. It was everything about him.

And her.

And them.

Oh my gosh, she wasn't ready for the feelings that laid

siege to her heart, but now that they were there, how could she ever push them away?

They drove in companionable silence, sipping at their cocoa, chatting occasionally but mostly keeping to their own thoughts until suddenly, Matt gasped and pointed out the front window toward the sky. "Look! I was hoping with it being this cold tonight we'd get a good show."

Brenna leaned forward to study the night sky. The stars were now joined by a fantastic light show comprised of bright greens, blues, and even pink. It was so beautiful it took her breath away. She'd hoped to see the Northern Lights in their full glory, but had only once caught a fleeting glimpse at the far edge of the horizon. What she was looking at now covered the whole sky.

Immediately, Matt pulled to the side of the road and stopped his truck. He reached behind the seat and grabbed a blanket, then opened his door and hopped out. "C'mon, you. You can't watch it properly sitting inside a vehicle."

She was still sitting in awed silence as Matt ran around to her door and yanked it open.

"What are we doing?" she protested. "I was finally starting to thaw out from skating."

"We don't want to miss this," he said, offering her his hand to help her down.

We. She liked being part of a *we.* A good one. Not *we* are terrified or *we* are hurt, but *we* are enjoying one of nature's most beautiful natural wonders.

She accepted his hand, hers shaking as she did—maybe from the cold or maybe from the hugeness of this moment.

Matt raced around his truck and opened the tailgate, then smoothed the blanket out in the bed. Before she could even attempt to hop up herself, he'd lifted her up and set her back down on their makeshift stargazing couch.

"You've never seen a true Alaskan aurora borealis until you've sat out on the edge of the city wrapped in a blanket watching it dance across the sky," he said after plunking down beside her.

"And it's extra cold tonight, so do you mind if we sit like this?" He opened his legs and motioned for her to crawl between them so he could hug her from behind and they could both enjoy the full warmth of the blanket. At first she was afraid to relax completely, but within minutes she'd leaned back into him and let him use the blanket and his own body heat to keep her warm.

In all her life, she couldn't remember anyone holding her like this. It made her feel safe and cared for, and she found herself wishing he'd never let go.

Brenna lifted her eyes and smiled to herself as she watched the colors undulating in waves across the sky. It was so quiet and peaceful that she felt as if they might be the only two people in the entire world and that this display had been made just for this moment, just for them. The cold air kissed her cheeks, but the rest of her was completely warm, wrapped in Matt's arms.

He leaned down and whispered in her ear. "Can you hear it?"

"Hear what?" She shivered as the feel of his warm breath caressed her earlobe. They were so close, and she wasn't running away. Maybe he'd kiss her again. Maybe this time she'd enjoy it.

"The lights," he said with an undeniable smile in his voice. "If you listen, sometimes you can hear them hissing as they move."

Brenna held her breath and sat perfectly still, waiting for that unmistakable S sound to find her. Finally, she gasped aloud as she thought she heard something whispering in the sky. "I think I can hear it!"

They sat together starting upward for what seemed like an eternity. Brenna wished it could be. Here in this silent place, no one would ever hurt her again.

But then her jaw clashed again and again as a wicked shiver rocked her body. "I guess we should get going before we both freeze to death." Even her words didn't sound convincing as she spoke them aloud.

His arms tightened and the side of his jaw pressed against her head. "You don't sound entirely certain. As for me? I could sit here forever with you. Just like that."

She gave her head a slow shake and tucked herself even deeper into his embrace even more. "You're right. Let's stay for a few more minutes. It's not like this kind of thing happens every day."

"Yes, a show this good is a once per season kind of thing. If that," Matt said with a dreamy sigh.

She chose not to tell him she hadn't been talking about the lights.

CHAPTER 15

Two more weeks slipped by. Brenna filled her time in the kitchen and with Matt, who came by more and more these days. True to his word, he hadn't tried to kiss her again, and she loved the delicious tension it created between them. She also loved that he was willing to wait to make her comfortable, no matter how uncomfortable it might make him.

Today was the day before Thanksgiving. Even though Matt's parents had invited her for their family meal, she'd stayed behind at the ranch to prepare the big feast for the staff and residents. Kate had offered to take her for a ride to give her a little break before the big show tomorrow, and for that Brenna was extremely grateful.

"You and Matt seem to have worked things out," Kate

said as she prepared to re-shoe one of the horses. "I don't think I've ever seen him look so happy. *Or you.*"

Brenna's cheeks flushed with embarrassment until she realized she had absolutely nothing to shame her in this situation. She was the happiest she could ever remember, and if Matt was, too, all the better. She smiled as she brushed Buddy's mane with firm hands. "We're just taking it slow to see what happens. So far, so good."

"I think I know what's going to happen," Kate teased.

Brenna laughed and resisted the urge to throw the brush at her friend.

Kate never pushed—just offered an ear to listen as needed whenever Brenna would hang out at the stables. It was part of the reason why she felt so at home at the ranch. Kate had become almost like her Alaskan sister—and lately she got along much better with her substitute sister than the real one, it seemed.

Brenna stopped brushing for a moment as she thought, but Buddy promptly put an end to that. He turned and nudged her hand with his nose, then promptly went back to eating. "Buddy, you're such a needy boy. Don't worry, I'm going to keep brushing." She laughed and shook her head at the horse who seemed to think he was the boss.

"Are you going to ask him out to the next barn dance? It'll be right around Christmas, you know and very romantic with all that mistletoe and what not," Kate told her. "I've heard that's one of the biggest ones this ranch hosts, and that even people from town can buy tickets to come out to it. The money is donated to charities that work with rescue horses."

Brenna looked over Buddy's back toward Kate in the next stall. "Liz mentioned something about that, and I was here for the last one. Although just barely." She remembered the fact that Ellie had a huge breakthrough at the last dance. Would this one provide her turn? And would she be ready?

She shook her head decisively. No, she still needed more time. The dance would be too much pressure. "I don't think so. I mean, I'm going to be busy making the food for it, and somehow that's going to be even bigger than this week with Thanksgiving. No, I already feel behind just thinking about it. I'll probably even have to put a few of you to work to help me get it all done on time."

Kate whipped her head up with a look of abject horror. "Um, I don't think I'd be able to help much. My cooking skills are more along the line of warming up a can of soup or picking up a phone to call for pizza. I'm sure all our guests would end up with some kind of food poisoning if you let me near anywhere near the kitchen."

Brenna laughed, grateful Kate had taken hold of the topic change. "I promise you won't have to do anything but follow my simple directions. I just need more hands and some good company. It would be great if you could help out tomorrow some, too."

Kate cleared her throat but didn't' speak.

"No pressure," Brenna quickly added.

"No, it's cool." Kate put on her brightest smile. "But I refuse to take responsibility if anyone ends up in the hospital."

They laughed and chatted about idle things as they both got the horses brushed and tucked in for the night. Brenna enjoyed the simple nature of this friendship. It didn't demand or force anything. She'd even grown accustomed to Kate's impromptu hugs, too.

Brenna hadn't had many true friends, but she considered Kate among them.

Over the years she'd become an expert at pretending her home life was perfect, never letting any friend get too close that they'd find out the truth. And, to be honest, she'd never let herself trust anyone enough that she could have ever talked about it with them. She'd been taught from an early age to keep her mouth closed and to never let anyone into the horrible world that hid inside her home.

When Brenna would go to school with bruises on her body, she always had perfect excuses to explain them away. So many times she would pray her teachers or someone would question her home life, but no one ever did. No one ever seemed to be willing to believe her perfect father could possibly be anything but what the world saw. He'd trained them all well. Especially his family.

Her phone vibrated in her pocket with a call from Matt. They hadn't talked since the previous evening when they'd caught each other up on their respective days, and she looked forward to catching up with him.

Except it wasn't him on the other end of the line.

It was her sister Olivia.

She hit the ignore button, again washed with guilt because she knew she wasn't being fair to her family back home. It just seemed that every time she talked to either her mother or her sister, the shared weight of their hurt suffocated her.

Maybe Brenna was being selfish, but she needed to be alone to do this. And all her life she'd been made to feel like she had no control over anything—the lies that were told, the moods in the house, or even the life she could present to the world.

Coming to Alaska was her chance to have control, and she couldn't give it up now. Not when she saw the strides she was making toward a better future. A better Brenna.

Her phone buzzed again. This time with a call from her mother.

She peeked up and caught Kate looking at her as she leaned against the stall door. "Your mom?" Kate knew there were some problems between Brenna and her mother but didn't know the full extent.

"Yeah, and my sister, too. I'll call them back once I'm back in my cabin. No sense making you listen to our arguments." She tried to laugh it off, but Kate knew her better than that.

"I know it isn't any of my business, but just remember that you only get one mom. One sister. Some people don't even get that."

Brenna thought she might have seen a flicker of a tear fall onto Kate's face, but the other woman jerked her head away before she could tell for sure.

"No matter what happened in the past, don't throw that away. It's too special," Kate concluded before disappearing into another stall, leaving Brenna standing on her own inside the stable.

Her stomach immediately clenched with guilt. Kate had mentioned one other time when they'd been in the stable together something about her own mom's health failing. She wasn't sure exactly what was happening with her, but Brenna knew it had to be so hard for Kate to see her suffering.

And here Brenna was acting like her family didn't matter, that she wasn't blessed to have them in her life. That she didn't care about them getting better, too.

Her phone vibrated again, but this time it was a text.

From her mother.

Her mom hardly ever texted because her father hadn't allowed it when he was living and she hadn't picked up since his death. Whatever this was, it must be serious.

Brenna's breath caught and her hands shook as the words of her mother's carefully constructed message jumped out at her: *Some man was here today asking questions about the night your dad died. He's found out where you are. I promise I didn't tell him, but he's on his way to Alaska.*

CHAPTER 16

BRENNA WAS ON CONSTANT WATCH OVER THE NEXT FEW days. There was a man who wanted to know more about her father's death, and he was coming to find her.

He knew. Or at the very least suspected.

And just as she'd started to enjoy her life for perhaps the first time ever. Just as things were working their way toward perfect, her past came calling.

When nobody new showed up at the ranch after several days, she began to rest easy. Had her mother misunderstood what the man had said? Or worse, was she making it all up to try to force Brenna to come back home before she was ready?

Whatever the case, he hadn't come.

This left her free to enjoy the holidays with her new

Alaskan friends and colleagues. Little by little, they had all started to become a family—the kind of family where no one hurt each other or guilt-tripped each other. It was truly the best.

She laughed as Matt walked into the living room of his parents' house wearing an oversized Santa hat and the ugliest sweater she'd ever seen. She sat cross-legged on the floor and pulled decorations out of a box, setting them up on the coffee table for his mom to sort from her place on the couch. Cynthia was still taking things easy after her surgery, so Brenna and Matt had volunteered to take the lead this year on decorating. Apparently, it all had to be done on that specific day as part of a long-standing Sanders family tradition.

"On the first day of Christmas," Matt sang out loud and off-key.

"Hey!" Brenna cried. "According to that song, there are only twelve days of Christmas. You told me the Sanders celebrate all twenty-five."

"That's right," his mom said. "I loved the Advent calendar growing up, and I love it still. You should find our family's calendar soon if you keep looking through those boxes, and when you do, why don't you do the honors of opening our first cubby this year?"

"Sounds like a great idea!" Matt's father, Michael, called from the kitchen where he was prepping a feast of roast chicken and root vegetables for them to enjoy once the decorating was finished.

And, oh, would they need it! Brenna was sure she'd never seen so many Christmas decorations in her life. It seemed like way more than would fit in their cozy home, but she was looking forward to being proven wrong and seeing the final display.

"Mom, put that down!" Matt cried as he rushed over to take the small box of ornaments his mother held as she pulled herself to her feet. "You know you aren't supposed to be lifting anything. Looks like someone is going on the naughty list."

Cynthia scowled at him and pulled the box out of her hands. "Seriously, Matt. This box only weighs about two pounds. Stop hovering."

"I'm not hovering, Mom. I'm just doing what the doctor told us. You are supposed to be taking it easy and not lifting anything. If you sit on the chair and just tell us where you want things, we will do it for you."

Matt's mom closed her eyes and took a deep breath. Brenna had to laugh at the exasperation she could feel ebbing forth from the poor woman. "Matthew James, I love you with all my heart, but you're driving me crazy. I'm not going to sit in a chair and do nothing while you two do everything. My surgery was more than a month ago. You can't treat me with kiddie gloves forever."

Matt glanced toward Brenna. "I'm not buying that. Are you?"

Brenna laughed as Cynthia sighed again.

"The doctor said six weeks," he pointed out. "Has it been six weeks? No."

"That's it, I'm going to get your father to throw you out that door." She turned and smiled sweetly at Brenna. "But Brenna can stay. She's actually being helpful and is always such a joy."

Brenna laughed out loud, then covered her mouth when she looked over at Matt.

He stood with his hands on his hips and his mouth hanging open, his Santa hat now looking completely out of place on his head. "Well, if you end up back in the hospital for Christmas, then don't blame me."

Matt's dad walked in with a tray of hot cocoa and cups for everybody. "Who am I throwing out?" he asked with a chuckle.

Cynthia groaned. "I'll give him one more chance. *One* more chance."

Brenna took a quick sip of cocoa, then set to work arranging the nativity scene in the center of the dining room table as instructed. As they worked, Brenna watched Matt patiently taking orders from his mom while they both teased each other left and right. Every now and then, they'd share memories from Christmases past as they examined various ornaments and found the perfect place for each on the large fir tree in the corner of the living room.

It had been a few weeks since the night he'd taken her skating, and they'd spend every day since talking on the phone and texting. Some evenings he would drive out to the ranch and they'd go for a ride or just walk around the grounds.

She still couldn't let herself go completely, still had so much work to do on herself.

But she was getting there, and Matt had made the impossible a very real—and achievable—thing. No matter what happened between them, she'd always be grateful, always think fondly of their time together, of his patience and kindness and willingness to help.

"Brenna?" Matt's mother said in a way that implied she'd tried to get her attention more than once.

Brenna shook away her thoughts. Why did it feel like she was composing a breakup speech in her head when she was otherwise content in the moment? "Yes?" she asked as sweetly as she could manage.

Cynthia patted the couch beside her and motioned for Brenna to sit. "I wanted to ask if you would spend Christmas Day with us. Matt mentioned that you might like to come, but if you have other plans, I understand."

"Oh, Mrs. Sanders, thank you. I hadn't really thought about it much, but..."

The truth was, Christmas hadn't ever been something she enjoyed as a child since that meant her dad was home more and drinking to celebrate the season. She had no happy memories of the holiday, and it seemed so strange that she now had the chance to finally make some of her own.

Brenna looked over at Matt, who was watching her closely. He gave her a kind smile, letting her know he was okay with whatever she decided. He would never force her to do anything she didn't want to do. She knew that very well by now.

She bit her lip as she thought. Would spending Christmas together be too big a step in their relationship? Did it matter?

Matt's mom patted her on the arm. "You can let me know. Our home is always open to you, and we'd love to have you. Besides, with me out of the kitchen this year, that leaves Matt and Michael in charge, and by the smell of the smoke coming from the kitchen, I'm not holding out much hope for the food situation, then or now."

As Cynthia spoke, her husband walked out of the kitchen waving his hand to clear the smoke. "I think the chicken is done."

Brenna laughed as the smoke detector began to trill, and both men raced around opening doors and flapping dish towels to clear the kitchen of smoke.

It gave her the time she needed to think and to realize

that in order to work through the memories of her past, she needed to be willing to make new memories to replace them. As she looked around at this happy, *crazy* family in this modest home, she realized this was a great place to start.

"Cynthia, thank you again for the invite. I'd love to spend Christmas here with you all. But only if you agree to let me make the Christmas dinner."

Michael walked over and handed the oven mitts to her with a big grin on his face. "Not only do I agree, Brenna. I insist."

CHAPTER 17

Brenna invited Matt over to the ranch to work as her kitchen apprentice. Seeing as she didn't have much money, this would be the perfect gift for Cynthia. Today, she was teaching him how to make her now-famous fruit muffins.

It was *not* going well.

"No, Matt. That's too much flour!" She raced to the other side of the island and ripped the bag from his hands. White powder dusted the counter, his apron, and had somehow even managed to get on his nose.

"Whoa. I didn't realize it was going to pour out of there that fast. It looks so easy when you do it." He grinned at her, leaving her laughing as she tried to scoop some of the loose flour back into the bag. If he could do this much damage

with a bag of flour, God help them both when it was time to use the oven.

"Looks so easy, huh?" she teased. "You made tattooing look easy. How about I do your next one?" Before she could stop herself, she reached up to wipe the smudge of flour from his nose.

Matt flinched on mock pain. "Ahh, point taken."

They lingered close until Brenna cleared her throat and retreated toward the fridge. "Um, maybe we should start with something easier. How about scrambled eggs?"

Matt winced as she returned to his side, a carton of eggs in tow. "Brenna, I'm hurt. But if it's what you want, then prepare to eat the best scrambled eggs of your entire life."

She laughed again as he yanked the carton of eggs from her hands and grabbed a fresh mixing bowl from the stack on the counter. Brenna had always enjoyed cooking and baking, but she had to admit, this was probably the most fun she'd ever had in the kitchen. Matt seemed to be enjoying himself, too. She was pretty sure he'd even given up his shift today—and the money that came with it—just to spend this extra bit of time with her.

"By the way," he said casually, "I'm glad you agreed to spend Christmas with us, but I was wondering. How did it go when you told your mom and sister?" He lifted his bright eyes to study her between cracking eggs. Apparently, he planned to make a ten-egg omelet. Lord help them both.

Brenna shrugged and tried not to obsess over the bit of eggshell resting on top of a yolk in Matt's bowl. "I haven't told them yet, but I will... eventually. I don't see why they're making it this huge thing this year. Christmas was never a big deal for us growing up. I don't see why that's suddenly different now that I'm up here."

Matt's mouth opened and his eyebrows pulled together. "Not a big deal? Man, growing up in my house, if you didn't treat Christmas like a huge deal you'd have been disowned. You know my mom would do it, too. She'd toss me right out on the streets in the middle of winter without a second thought."

A sudden lump formed in her throat as she thought back to a Christmas that she'd spent in the hospital so many years ago. It was actually one of her best memories because at least she was out of the house. Last year, she'd locked herself in her room and refused to talk to anybody, still unwilling to admit that her father was really dead. That it had been...

"Is everything okay?" Matt said, sliding his hand across the counter to grace her hand with his thumb.

"You know, I think decorating with you and your family might be one of my first happy Christmas memories ever."

Matt balked. *"Ever?"*

"Christmas meant more things for my dad to throw and kick around. It meant more drinking and even more pretending to be a happy family than usual." Her eyes glassed over as she recalled a particularly upsetting Christmas three years ago. "One year, he got so mad at us, he grabbed the tree and threw it out the window. It was the last time we had a tree."

She lifted her gaze and smiled sadly. "Christmas just wasn't much fun for us."

His eyes hardened as he watched her. "That's awful, Brenna. I'm so sorry."

She laughed bitterly. "Yeah, but it is what it is. I can't change the past."

Matt squeezed her hand and pulled her to his chest for a hug. "But today is a gift. That's why they call it the present. So Merry Christmas." His fingers moved up to trace along her cheek.

She shivered but didn't back away.

"I hate what he's done to you. And I wish I knew how to erase everything he did."

Brenna blinked hard to dry the wetness that blurred her vision. This was an important moment, and she wanted to see him. "You've already done more than you know, Matt. *So much.*"

As she looked up into the eyes that held so much concern and compassion, she desperately hoped he would kiss her. It had been more than three months since she'd first met him in the tattoo shop. They hadn't kissed since the day they'd made the snowman together—the day she ran away. He was waiting for her to tell him she was ready.

And, in that moment, she thought maybe she was.

No— she *knew.*

"Can you kiss me now?" she squeaked.

"I thought you'd never ask," came his throaty reply. His lips moved over hers in a featherlight touch, and this time she didn't run away.

"Doing okay?" he murmured against her cheek, which she took as an invitation to kiss him again.

And again. As her lips found Matt's, something inside her also clicked into place. Could she finally be healing? Had she finally learned to trust? To love?

Someone cleared her throat in the entryway, and Brenna reluctantly pulled away from Matt. His skin looked raw from their kiss, and she wondered if hers did, too.

"Hi, Elizabeth Jane," she said, covering her mouth with both hands and trying not to blush any more than she already was.

"Hi, Brenna Barry," Liz said without any of her usual bluster or zeal. "I'm sorry to interrupt, but there's someone here. And he's demanding to talk to you. Do you want me to send him away?"

Brenna flinched as if the words had physically slammed into her. She knew exactly who had come to see her even though she'd so desperately prayed this day would never come. And as much as she didn't want to, she knew she had to talk to him—otherwise he'd keep hunting her down until she finally opened up. No sense running from the inevitable.

Not anymore.

"You look worried. Do you know who it is?" Matt asked, dropping his voice to a whisper.

Her world started to spin, and she knew everything she'd been trying to run away from had finally cornered her. There was no escape now. How could she ever have believed she could get away?

All she could do was nod, knowing as soon as she voiced the truth, everything would change. Matt wouldn't look at her with love in his eyes anymore. Liz would probably fire her, and this man just might put her in jail.

Still, she needed to tell them before that man outside could do it for her.

She took a deep breath, clenched her eyes shut, and said, "He's here because he knows I'm the one who killed my father."

CHAPTER 18

BRENNA KEPT HER EYES SEALED TIGHT. SHE COULDN'T BEAR to see Matt and Liz's horrified expression, nor could she stand to witness the exact moment they both decided to be done with her. Finally her past had caught up with her, and it was exactly what she deserved—what she'd always deserved.

When she opened her eyes again, she saw both of her former friends staring at her with open mouths. Apparently, they'd been trying to say more for a while now, but Brenna had become an expert at blocking out voices she didn't want to hear.

She wished she could cry, but she didn't feel guilty about what she had done. She only felt bad that she had let down the people who had trusted her, who had wanted to help her.

"Brenna, what happened? What are you talking about?" Matt's voice was low, his eyes cold. All this time, Brenna had been trying to find a way to trust him, and now he knew that she was the one who could never be trusted. There was an evil that lived somewhere inside of her.

Even Liz had taken a step back when Brenna made her big revelation.

"You heard me. I killed my dad, and I'm not sorry," she said, clenching her teeth, willing herself to feel some kind of pain instead of this maddening blankness.

"Brenna, no." Liz brought a hand to her chest. Was she surprised or only pretending? Shouldn't the therapist have told her everything by now?

But, oh, she didn't know, either. Brenna had locked that part of herself away and figured if she hid it long enough that part of her past might just disappear altogether. How wrong she'd been.

"It's true he had an accident, but I'm the one who made it happen," she said, trying to detach herself as she revisited the events of that night. "It had been a couple years since I graduated and moved out. And I never came back to visit, either. The only time I went anywhere near that house was when I knew for a fact he would be at work. The rest of the time, I made my mom and sister come to me."

Brenna turned and walked over to the window that looked out to the stables. She could see Buddy standing there and, as she watched, he lifted his head and stared directly into her eyes. He was saying goodbye to her, too.

"That night was different, though. My sister kept texting *SOS* and when I tried to call her, she told me that dad was going to kill mom and maybe her, too, if I didn't get there fast." She wrapped her arms around herself and leaned her forehead onto the cold window frame. The memories of that night flooded her mind, and she knew it was time to face it. No matter how far she ran, it was always going to be there.

"And so even though I was scared out of my mind, I went. But when I got there, the door was locked and the house was dark. I tried to call the police, but as soon as I hung up with the dispatcher, I heard a gunshot go off inside. That's when I stopped thinking altogether. I was going to do whatever it took to save my mom and sister. So, I ran to the back and broke the window in the bathroom that I'd always used to escape when I lived at home."

Matt came over and placed a hand on her shoulder. He didn't say anything, just waited for her to finish.

"I landed on my sister, who was hiding in the bathtub, crying hysterically. But I didn't have time to ask her for more details. I just ran toward the sound like I had a death wish. Maybe I did.

"My mom was lying in a fetal position on the ground, but thank God, she was still breathing and there wasn't much blood. Yet. But he was sitting on top of her, hitting her over and over again with the butt of that gun..."

Brenna's voice caught as a sob tore from her throat. Every emotion from that night was replaying in her body now. She'd never told the full story before. Even her mother and sister never talked about what happened that night after it was all over—never asked her to explain how it had happened.

It felt like a relief to get all the ugly words out of her. Now that she'd started to recount the events of that night, she couldn't bring herself to stop. Faster and faster they came, tumbling one over the other, racing toward the horrifying ending.

She clenched her eyes shut again as she remembered. This was the most important part, and she had to get it right. "I'll never forget the growl that tore from his throat as I ran over and kicked him again and again as hard as I could. He sounded more like an animal than a man. Even over all the years when he'd beaten me and I was sure he was going to kill me, I had never heard any sound like that."

She swallowed again, trying to calm her racing heart. "Then he grabbed my leg and yanked me down to the ground with him. My mom was unconscious, and my sister was still hiding. I didn't know how long it would be until the police came. It was all up to me now."

Brenna paused for a moment and got her breathing

under control. Now it was time to say the hardest words of all—the reason she even had to make her confession, the important fact that transformed this episode from any other day of her life into the worst and best one combined.

"He stopped hitting me long enough to grope for his gun on the carpet. It made a clicking sound, and for a moment I thought I was already dead. But then I realized I wasn't, not yet, and that I had to save my family from this monster. All the anger at what we had suffered took over my body and, suddenly, I found myself leaping at him with more strength than I ever knew I had. It was like I wasn't even in control anymore, and that was okay.

"I grabbed his hands, knowing full well he was too drunk to put up much of a fight. He shot and the bullet zipped past us both. That's when I knew he wasn't going to back down, and that I had to make a choice. Fast. When the gun clicked again, I pulled it from his hands and fired it straight into his chest."

Her entire body shook as the memories flooded her mind. When she turned to face Matt and Liz, she squared her shoulders, ready for them to condemn her.

Instead, Matt pulled her into his arms, holding her against his strong chest as she finally let the years of fear and pain flow out of her.

Liz came over and wrapped her arms around them both. "Brenna, if you would have done anything differently, then someone else would have died. You're not a criminal. You're a hero."

Brenna shook her head and finally began to cry. "I don't know why that man is here, but I assume it's to punish me for what I did. The police didn't ask too many questions before ruling it self-defense. Maybe I should have been in jail this whole time. Whatever it is, I'm ready to face what I deserve."

Matt pulled her to his chest and forced her to look directly into his eyes as he swore, "Well, whoever this guy is, he's going to have to get through me first."

CHAPTER 19

BRENNA MARCHED OUTSIDE WITH LIZ ON ONE SIDE AND Matt on the other. Her friends hadn't backed away when they learned her ugly truth. If they understood, maybe the man waiting in the stables for her could, too. It would be easier now that she had her friends at her side.

"Are you sure you're ready for this?" Matt asked as he squeezed her side tight.

"Yeah, I can still tell him to get out of here," Liz reminded her.

"He'll just come back," Brenna answered as she set her features into a blank, determined mask. "I need to do this eventually, so I might as well do it now."

"We'll be right there for you the whole time," Matt said, but Brenna was already rehearsing her words in her head, already telling herself that she could do this, that things would be all right soon.

"I was beginning to think you wouldn't come," a tall man wearing an inexpensive looking suit said from where he was standing near Buddy. Brenna instantly disliked him.

"Well, you were wrong. Now tell me, what do you want?"

He clucked his tongue and kicked off from the wall to draw closer. Motioning to Brenna's friends, he said, "Nuh uh, we do this alone, or we don't do it all."

"She's good with not doing it at all," Liz interjected, putting a hand on each of her hips and storming toward the intruder. "You're the one pushing this issue."

"So then you prefer not to make a statement in regards to my investigation?" He pulled his phone out of a coat pocket and tapped at the screen. "Interesting."

"What's this about?" Matt demanded, but the investigator ignored him.

He focused his gaze solely on Brenna. "Committed so many crimes you can't even keep them all straight. And here I thought murder was bad enough on its own." He laughed to himself, then pointed to Liz and Matt each in turn. "I'm serious. They need to go."

"No way!" Matt shouted.

Brenna placed a calming hand on his arm, noticing how

he shook with rage in that moment. "It's okay. I can handle this."

"But you don't need to handle it by yourself," Matt insisted as Liz shot a searing glance at Brenna's interrogator.

"You're the one who told me I'm strong," Brenna reminded him. "I think you even used the word 'unbreakable.' Now give me a chance to prove it."

Matt looked like he was going to argue further, but Liz nodded and pushed him back toward the house. "We'll just be inside if you need us at all. Promise you'll call if you need us."

"I will. Thank you." Brenna watched her two friends retreat into the warmth of the main ranch house, of her kitchen. She turned back to the stranger. "Okay, we're alone. Now what can I do for you?"

The man grinned, obviously finding it amusing that she wasn't backing away from him. Could his large, probing eyes see right through her? If so, had he seen how desperate she was that night? How much she'd suffered in silence before finally taking action?

"Good. Let's cut right to the chase." He groped about in his pants pocket and extracted a small case. "Name's Willy Hardy, Private Investigator. Your father's life insurance company hired me to do some digging into the unusual circumstances of his death. Here's my card."

He handed her a thin bit of cardstock with his name and

details printed on the surface. She felt like tearing it up in front of him, but instead jammed it in her pocket and waited for what he planned to say next.

"Where were you living when your father died?"

"In an apartment a few miles away from my parents' home."

"How often did you visit your family after you moved out?"

"Not often. I didn't much care for my father."

"So you're just going to offer me motive without any digging on my part, I see. You're making this too easy on me, Ms. Barry."

"I have nothing to hide from you. The police investigated everything that happened that night, and I don't understand why you've been hired to look into it. What can it possibly prove?"

He shook his head at her as if she were a petulant child gearing up for a tantrum. "Nope, I'm the one asking questions here. Now tell me why you didn't—in your own words —much care for your father."

"You know nothing about what we went through that night, what we went through *many* nights." With her entire body shaking, she turned to walk away from the man, opening Buddy's stall door to let him out. This man had sent her friends away because he must have known it would be easier to get under her skin. But she still had one friend nearby, and she was going to make sure she had him at her side.

Unfortunately, the interrogator followed her without hesitation, even reaching up to stroke Buddy's side. "Nice looking horse."

Brenna glared at him over Buddy's back as she hoisted the saddle up. The ranch staff tended to keep conversations focused on the patients rather than themselves, but she knew enough to know that Liz's husband Dorian had been a P.I. in a past life. She hoped he wasn't as obnoxious as this guy. He certainly wasn't now, but...

She focused her attention back on the man before her, Will Hardy. She wanted to take the pitchfork beside her and chase him out of the ranch for good, but she held back. He already suspected the worst of her.

Obviously, though, Buddy could sense that Will wasn't a good man, either, because her loyal friend snorted loudly and directly into the man's face, forcing him to reach up and wipe at his face.

Brenna chuckled to herself as she pulled the strap tight on Buddy's saddle.

"I'm glad you find that amusing," he said, picking back up where he left off. "Now, you say I have no idea what you went through. Tell me. That's why I'm here."

"Is it? You're here to understand?" she demanded,

steeling herself. "Because it seems like you already think I'm guilty."

"Then prove to me you're not. Why were you at the house that night? Were you there against your father's wishes?"

"I came because my sister invited me."

"You answered one question, but not the other. Why is that?"

She clenched her jaw tight. "I have no idea what my father wanted. He was often too drunk to know for himself."

"I see the disgust on your face. You don't like people who drink, yet it's okay to get cozy with a drug dealer?"

"Leave my friends out of this. You're the one who sent them away. Not me."

"But first you sent yourself away. Didn't you? As far from the scene of the crime as you could get. Why Alaska, Brenna?"

"I came to work at Memory Ranch."

"Not because you needed a cover? How long have you known Matt Sanders? Did you know him when you still lived in Florida?"

"No, this has nothing to do with Matt, and you know that."

"I do, do I? Well, do you know he was present at the scene of an arson back in 2017? That somebody died in that fire?"

This caught Brenna off guard. "What?"

"And does he know you killed your father?"

Brenna's head spun. Matt said he'd never hurt anyone—joked about it even. Could what this pushy investigator was claiming be true? She glared at him even harder, wishing Buddy would step on the man's foot and crush it.

He nodded and tapped on his phone again. "So you're both liars and you're both murderers. Seems like you two are a match made in heaven."

Brenna had a hard time catching her breath as the world continued to spin around her. She needed to talk to Matt, but no. He'd lied to her. In wake of this new revelation, she didn't trust herself to talk about the night of her father's death any longer. Her head was too foggy, and with her luck, Will Hardy would confuse her further and convince her to confess to motives she didn't have and crimes she didn't commit.

He cocked a smile at her, knowing he had her cornered—cornered but not trapped. "Not going to say anything else?"

"I have nothing else to say to you," she said coldly, then put her foot into the stirrup and threw her leg over Buddy's back.

The man stepped back out of the way as she started to walk the horse out of the stable. "Sure, run away, but just know that I'll be back."

Brenna didn't listen to another word as she kicked her

heels in and let Buddy take her away. She couldn't believe she'd ever thought her nightmare had come to an end the night her father died. And she couldn't believe she'd allowed herself to trust someone who had never deserved it in the first place.

Perhaps if she ran fast enough, all the pain would fly away with the swirling snow and raging winds that filled the sky. Perhaps if she ran far enough, she'd finally get away from herself.

CHAPTER 20

THE COLD STUNG BRENNA'S EYES AS SHE LET BUDDY RACE down the trail as fast as his legs could carry them in this kind of weather. The heavy snowfall combined with the already thick blanket coating the earth made the trails slick with slush, but Buddy's footing was sure. Even in her darkest moment, she would never do anything to risk injuring the horse who had become her most honest and constant friend.

"Why does everyone make it their mission to hurt me, Buddy?" she shouted into the swirling wind. "The moment I start to trust again is the very moment I learn that I can never let myself be close to anyone ever again. Well, anyone besides you." She laughed bitterly, leaning forward in the saddle and letting her body relax as the trees flew by in a blur. She let the tears roll down her cheeks, not even caring that they would likely freeze into little icicles.

The investigator would be back with more questions, ready to break her in any way he could. The worst part was Brenna wasn't even sure she knew what the answers were anymore. Everything that had happened that night was a blur, and now the seeds of doubt had been planted about her mom's insurance policy. Why would they even need to hire a P.I. to look into things a full year after her father's funeral?

"Just keep going, Buddy. Take me as far away from all of this as we can go."

Together, they raced over the open trail with the snow starting to come down harder, leaving wet streaks on her cheeks that covered the falling tears. The cold flakes were like a balm to her battered soul as they touched her skin. She knew she should turn around and head back before the snow got too heavy, but she also couldn't risk running into the P.I. again—or worse, Matt.

He'd seemed so kind and gentle, patient with her, but all the while he'd been harboring an even darker past than he'd let on. He had set a fire and killed someone, and he was never going to tell her. People couldn't change, after all.

Her father had beaten them mercilessly for years. He never became kind. Brenna struggled with letting others in, but she would never make that mistake again. And Matt was a criminal in the past and a liar now. Maybe he even still dealt drugs behind her back. Maybe everyone knew and secretly laughed at Brenna.

Yes, Buddy was the only friend she needed now. If they just kept running, they could find a new life where no one knew their names or histories. She could start over. Be more careful this time. Maybe if she ended up far enough away from her home in Florida and from the ranch in Anchorage, the hurting would finally stop.

After another hour or more of riding, Brenna suddenly realized the snow had fallen so thick and fast, all of the usual landmarks she used to mark her trail were now buried beneath a fresh layer of white. The ground was completely white. The air was completely white. She and Buddy were the only speck of color for what was probably miles. She'd been so preoccupied by her feelings that she'd forgotten to be safe.

She stopped Buddy and just sat for a few moments, staring ahead into the falling snow as it swirled around her in a mass of confusion, flakes going in every direction. It matched how she felt inside with her thoughts in a messy, senseless jumble.

And, like the snowfall, her thoughts wouldn't stop pummeling her, either. Could she think clearly enough to get her and Buddy home safely? She'd never forgive herself if something happened to this sweet and generous horse because of her carelessness.

"All right, let's go home." Brenna needed to be confident for him, otherwise they'd both panic. She pulled on the reins to turn him around, moving him through the increasingly deep snow around them. But no matter how hard she tried to find them, Buddy's tracks were buried almost the second he put them down. The only thing breaking up the continuous wall of white were various copses of trees, which she could only see once they were very close. She didn't know which trees lined the trail and which were part of the forest. She had no idea which direction to go, how to get them out of this mess.

But it was up to her to figure it out.

"It must be this one, Buddy," she said, nudging his side with her boot and tugging on the reins decisively—even though she had no idea if her directions were right.

"I'm sure this is the way we came," she said anyway. Her voice wavered as the wind slammed into her, chapping her cheeks and chilling her bones. How could she not have realized how bad of an idea riding off during an impending snow storm would be? The combined effect of the wind and snow made it impossible to see in front of them, but she had to keep pressing forward. Their lives might depend on it.

Brenna yanked off one of her mitts off and reached into her pocket for her cell phone. If she could get a hold of Liz, maybe she could give her some better directions or even bring a snow machine out to find her. Her stiff fingers groped about furiously, but her pocket was empty. She'd left her phone in the kitchen, forgetting to grab it between making her confession to Matt and Liz and going outside to meet Will Hardy.

It served her right.

And if it had just been her stuck out in this storm, maybe she would have given up trying right then and there.

But she couldn't do that to Buddy. Maybe the horse's instincts would kick in and he'd find the way back for her. She could only hope that he knew what to do. He was an Alaskan horse, after all.

They continued to work their way slowly across the fields, the trails, whatever ground they came upon. The wind picked up more and more with every step they took. Brenna pulled her collar up higher to try shielding her cheeks from the piercing sting of the air. She'd never been so cold in all her life, and even now the chill dug deeper and deeper into her body.

No one knew where she'd gone, and she had no idea how long she could be out in these temperatures like this. She only had her jacket, mittens, and hood to keep the cold out.

Maybe if she leaned forward and wrapped her arms around Buddy's neck, she'd get some warmth from him. She had to do something because with every passing second, the chattering of her teeth grew louder and more violent.

But, no. It was not enough. Not when she was already so cold.

She needed to get down from his back and find some shelter from the wind, if only for a moment, if only for a little while.

She searched anxiously for a group of trees or anything she could use to shield herself. Finally, an extra-large pine came into view, and she leaped down from Buddy with great relief...

Until she landed on what should have been soft ground. Her legs were so frozen over already that they wouldn't hold her up, causing her to fall into the deep snow. Still, she had to fight. She dragged herself over to the tree and leaned into it, letting it provide some shelter from the bitter wind whipping all round her.

As she tucked her legs up to her chin and wrapped her arms around them to try and keep herself as small as possible, she started to cry again. When she'd run away from the ranch in tears, she'd wanted to just get lost and not ever be found again.

Now that was exactly what had happened, and she'd never been so scared in all her life.

CHAPTER 21

BRENNA COULD HEAR HER MOTHER SOBBING, SHRIEKING, begging for him to stop—but his cruelty was unrelenting that night. He was on top of her, bashing her face in with the gun, blood going everywhere. Brenna was frozen in place, only able to watch as he beat the life from her. Spit flew from his mouth and his knuckles turned white as he squeezed her windpipe.

Suddenly a fire lit inside her, and the lapping flames freed her arms and then her legs.

"Get off her, you disgusting piece of garbage," Brenna yelled as she flung herself at him and knocked him to the ground.

But he still had the gun. He fired. Missed. Let a new bullet into the chamber.

"I hate you. I hate you. I hate you!" She kept saying the words over and over as they struggled for control of the gun.

He sneered at her, his eyes full of rage. "You girls have never appreciated anything I do for you, and I'm done putting up with it." His words hissed out between his clenched teeth as he pushed her and she fell back.

She had to keep fighting. She wasn't going to let him win.

Not this time. Not any time ever again.

Over and over, the bullet fired on loop. Brenna squeezed the trigger. Blood blossomed from his chest. He crumpled lifeless on the ground.

Rewind. Repeat.

Again, and again, and again.

But this time he wasn't dead. He reanimated like some kind of zombie, got up again, told her she was going to pay for this. He grabbed her by the arms and held her in a prison of flesh and blood, ready to exact his final revenge.

"No! No, let go! I hate you!" she screamed, but it was no use.

He shook her harder and harder still.

"Brenna!" a desperate voice called from somewhere in the distance, but it didn't belong to her father.

Her eyes flew open, and she saw Matt's face close to hers as he held her in his arms.

Wait, wasn't she supposed to be mad at him about something? She couldn't remember.

Was her father still nearby, or had he really died? She didn't know.

"Brenna, it's me!" Matt shouted over the wind. "You're safe. No one's going to hurt you."

She tried to move into his arms but her body seemed frozen to the spot. "Matt. I'm so cold." Her voice was weak. She didn't even know if he could hear her.

He stuck his flashlight in his pocket and reached out to her, easily lifting her into his arms.

She groaned as pain shot through her body.

"It's okay, Brenna. Just let me carry you. I'm going to get you warmed up," he promised. Matt held her tight as he stumbled through the snow toward Buddy and another horse that he must have been riding on his way to find her.

His eyes were burning with determination. He seemed so strong while she was so weak. "If I prop you up in the saddle, can you hold on and wait for me to get up behind you?"

"I can try." Her voice didn't even sound like her own.

Matt hefted her up onto his horse's back, and she slouched forward to hold on the best she could. His hand stayed on her leg, offering support as he hopped up behind her. Immediately, he pulled her back against him and wrapped his arms tightly around her.

This was it. She'd really been rescued, but as Matt kicked his heels in and called out to Buddy to follow, she had a hard time remembering how she'd ended up stranded outside and alone in a snow storm.

The longer they rode, the more she felt the beginnings of strength return to her limbs. Not enough—never enough —but she could at least speak and feel the searing pain that threatened to rip her apart.

"Poor Buddy," Brenna moaned. "He must be frozen." Her teeth chattered as she spoke, and the sound was strangled as she sucked in the cold air.

"Don't worry about Buddy. He's fine. Actually, he's the one who saved you. He found me as I was searching for you and brought me here. I don't think I would have found you in time, otherwise." His voice cracked. Maybe he was crying, but she couldn't look behind herself to check. She wasn't strong enough yet, and perhaps it didn't matter, either.

She had so much more to ask, so much more to say, but she couldn't remember what. The howling of the wind drowned out her thoughts. The sharp sting in her extremities made it hard to focus on anything but the pain. If she was so cold, then why did it burn?

Perhaps she would feel better if she just closed her eyes for a few seconds and allowed herself to rest...

BRENNA'S EYES SHOT OPEN. Somehow they were the only part of her that didn't hurt. Everything stung, burn, tingled, and ached, but at least she wasn't cold anymore. When she'd been trapped in the storm she had feared that even if she survived, she would never feel warmth again.

She struggled to sit up, but her body seemed to be just as weak as it was sore. Without realizing it, she moaned aloud as she fell back against her pillow.

"Brenna, are you all right?" Matt appeared from the edge of the room outside her vision and came to sit down beside her. "Do you need anything?"

Brenna pulled her eyebrows together in confusion as she tried figure out where she was and how she'd gotten here. Oh, great. Her brain hurt, too.

"Matt, why are you here? What's going on?" She begged him for answers, realizing then that she trusted him to make sense of all this, that he was the one who had rescued her from the snow.

"After you lost consciousness, I got you back to the ranch and called for an ambulance to get you to the hospital. We tried warming you up while we waited, but you never woke up. Not until now. You've been in the hospital overnight." He stroked her arm as he spoke to her. His touch didn't hurt —it felt comforting. It felt right.

"You stayed with me?" she squeaked, noticing now that the blackness of night had been replaced by the brightness of a new day. The threatening white of the snow had transformed into the protective blankets that encased her, brought warmth back into her bones.

"Of course, I did. I wasn't going to leave you here alone. They did some x-rays because we weren't sure if you'd fallen from Buddy or what had happened. They said they'd come and talk to us once you woke up."

Matt's concern was evident in every part of his body. Had he forgone sleep while he waited for her to awaken from hers?

Brenna squeezed her eyes shut as she tried to recall what had happened and why. "No, I didn't fall," she revealed to them both. "I just got down to try and get some shelter from the wind."

She fought through the pain to hoist herself into a sitting position so they could talk more easily. "Will they let me go home today?" she wanted to know.

"I don't know, but I'll stay with you until they do." Matt reached for her hand and gave it a squeeze.

Both of their heads turned toward the door as a doctor breezed into the room. "Ms. Barry, you had us all quite worried, but it looks like you're even tougher than we'd hoped."

Someone else had called her *Ms. Barry* recently, but who? The memory pricked at the edges of her consciousness, but she couldn't bring it into full focus.

"You did suffer from a mild case of hypothermia but we were able to get your body temperature warmed up quickly," the doctor continued, flipping a page on his chart. "Your x-rays revealed that nothing was broken...this time."

Matt's smile fell away as he looked to the doctor in confusion. "What do you mean *this time?*"

The doctor glanced at Brenna, waiting for her to give her consent for him to say more. But it was okay, right? Matt already knew about the abuse. None of this should come as a shock.

Did he know about her role in her father's death, too? She thought maybe she had confessed, but couldn't remember when or how he'd reacted. The fact that he was here with her now, that he'd rescued her last night, had to be a good sign.

When she nodded her approval, the doctor referenced the chart in his hands and said, "I'd say from the look of Ms. Barry's scans, she's had quite her share of broken bones. There are a lot of healed fractures and old breaks that are visible in the x-rays consistent with the signs of extended, prolonged physical abuse."

Brenna's eyes fell to the sheet pooled in her lap. She knew Matt would be upset, and she didn't want to see it. She hurt more than enough already.

"How many broken bones?" Matt didn't even attempt to conceal his anger as he demanded more.

At one time, she'd have lied as her father had trained her to do. She'd tell them she'd been in a car accident, that she'd misremembered and Buddy really had thrown her from his back. That's the kind of thing she'd always said before whenever anyone asked questions, but she didn't need to say it now. Her father couldn't hurt her anymore, and perhaps the truth would finally set her free.

With an inner strength that surprised even her, she lifted her eyes to meet Matt's and told her the secret she'd once worked so hard to hide. "I've had six broken ribs, broken my left arm twice, my collarbone, my ankle, a fractured pelvis, and a ruptured spleen. I think that's everything."

Matt shook and grew red with rage, but didn't say a word. There was nothing anyone could say. They all knew Brenna had been hurt far more than anyone deserved. When Matt asked for a moment and paced out into the hall, Brenna let go of the breath she hadn't realized she'd been holding.

If her father hadn't already been dead, she knew that Matt would have killed him with his bare hands. But he didn't have to—she'd already done the job for him.

CHAPTER 22

THE DOCTOR TALKED TO BRENNA FOR A LITTLE WHILE AND gave her a prescription for painkillers and a referral to a therapist. After a quick check of her vitals, he told her she'd be ready for discharge that same day. Brenna thanked him, and he left.

Now she sat up on the edge of the bed, still and silent, as she waited for Matt to come back and join her. She knew he couldn't have gone far, but still, he had vanished for the better part of half an hour. As she sat by herself, she tried to remember why she had been so upset the night before. Had it just been about her father, or had something new happened?

She remembered talking to Matt and Liz in the kitchen but couldn't remember what all she'd revealed. She also remembered another person, someone she didn't like very much calling her Ms. Barry and making her feel angry. The particulars would come back to her soon. She knew they would. Her brain just had to thaw out a little more. She had to move past the trauma of being lost in the storm to start piecing her thoughts back together regularly again.

Similar such short-term lapses had happened to her in the past following particularly cruel beatings from her father. Her therapist at the ranch called it compartmentalization and said it was a safety measure Brenna had unwittingly concocted to protect her brain.

The memories always came flooding back eventually, but not until she was ready to deal with them. Apparently, she wasn't yet ready to address whatever had happened the night before.

Still, she was tremendously curious and hoped the fog would clear soon.

At last Matt returned with a smile on his face and a cup of coffee in each hand. He handed one to her then sank onto the bed beside her, sitting close but not touching.

"Thanks for this," she said, lifting the cup to her lips with a grateful sigh.

Matt nodded as his features rearranged themselves into a grimace. "I knew he'd hurt you, Brenna. But I had no idea how badly. Why didn't you tell me?"

"Tell you what?" she asked with a bitter laugh. "That I spent a lot of time in hospitals growing up, being fixed back up after he hurt me, and everyone always believed the stories he gave them about an accident I'd had? No one ever questioned the great Patrick Barry. And if anyone suspected, they obviously didn't care enough to do anything about it."

Matt's hands tightened around his cup, and for a moment she feared the coffee would come sloshing out from the top. "You mean like your mother? Where was she during all of this?" His voice shook with anger. "What kind of a mother would let this happen?"

"She's not the one who hit me. He is," Brenna pointed out.

"But she let him. I just don't understand."

"I'm glad you don't," she said softly, truly meaning the words as she spoke them. "It means you've had a better life than I have so far."

They sat side by side in silence as they both considered this.

"Let's leave the past in the past," she said, offering her hand palm up which he accepted with an exhausted sigh. "We've both had hard times, but we have each other now. Things can be better."

She knew there was something else about Matt she'd recently learned, but what was it? Whatever it was, it couldn't be bad. This was her Matt, her kind, gentle Matt. He'd saved her, helped her heal, and maybe—just maybe—he even loved her.

His renewed smile told her all she needed to know. "I like the sound of that," he admitted. "I like it very much."

"Knock, knock." A familiar voice she couldn't quite place wafted over from the doorway.

They both turned toward the man waiting with a bouquet of half-brown flowers in the hall. He wore a suit but no tie, and his dark hair was in need of a trim.

"You again," Matt growled while Brenna tried to remember how she knew him. "Haven't you done enough damage already?"

"Ms. Barry, I was so sorry to hear about what happened the other night. You know, you wouldn't have had to go through all that if you'd just stayed and answered my questions."

"Questions?"

"Sure, don't you remember?"

"Will," she said. "Your name is Will Hardy. You're a P.I."

He made a little gun gesture with his free hand and pointed at Brenna. "Bingo. These are for you, by the way." He handed her the flowers, which were even uglier up close. Now it was all coming back to her. She had not enjoyed her last conversation with this man, and she wasn't sure she was ready for another.

"She's in the hospital, for crying out loud," Matt protested. "Don't you piranhas ever take any time off?"

"Not when we have a job to do. Give us a few minutes to

ourselves?" he asked Matt, who folded both arms over his chest and stared down the bridge of his nose at Mr. Hardy.

"No way. That did not end well the last time."

Will just shrugged. "Fine. Whatever." Yesterday he'd been adamant about talking to Brenna on her own. What had changed?

"What will it take to make you go away as fast as possible?" Brenna asked, glowering at the man with hate. He was looking into her father's death. She knew that much, but why?

"First, let's revisit what I know, then you can tell me the parts I'm missing." He pulled out his phone and read from the screen. "One, your parents took out a massive life insurance four years ago. Two, your father died during a domestic dispute one year ago. Three, your mother requested a lump payout of $250,000 one month ago. With me so far?"

Brenna nodded, unwilling to give anything away before she understood his angle.

Matt's eyes turned to hers, full of questions she couldn't yet answer.

Will Hardy paced to the other side of the room and narrowed his eyes first at Brenna and then Matt. "Insurance fraud is a very serious crime. As is murder. Oh, and hey, arson, too. So, tell me, which should we talk about first?"

Insurance fraud. She remembered that part now. The company had hired this oaf to investigate, but arson?

She looked toward Matt, who'd grown bright red with anger. "Get out of this room," he growled, shoving the other man in his chest. "And if I ever see you near Brenna again, you're going to be sorry."

The investigator chuckled and tapped something on his phone. "Adding assault to the list as well, I see. You picked a real winner, Ms. Barry. A real winner."

The cruel expression on his face showed that he considered Matt anything but.

Brenna, too.

"You might be able to intimidate other people with threats," Will Hardy said to Matt, "but you can't scare me off. I'm following the law and have every right to ask questions for my client."

Brenna's mind raced around in circles. She was so close to remembering. So close.

"And I have every right to protect my girlfriend from scum like you." It seemed Matt was ready to start pounding on the other man right there in the middle of her hospital room. But he was gentle, not violent like her father. He'd done drugs, but he'd never hurt anyone. He'd told her that much when...

Oh, my gosh.

Brenna's head reeled around the truth she'd learned the night before. Matt had done something terrible, and then he'd hid it from her. He was still hiding.

"You know," the investigator continued, "the past will always come back to haunt you unless you face up to the truth. If your mother is pulling something on my client, we'll find out. So you can keep hiding behind your boyfriend's threats, but someday I'll find out what happened. The police might have made a mess of the original investigation, but I won't make the same mistakes."

Matt pushed the man again, still holding him by the front of his coat. "Get out." He gave one final shove and let go, leaving Will to stumble awkwardly toward the door.

"You can't hide forever," he said on the way out the door.

Matt spun to face her, confusing marring his features. "Your mom took out an insurance policy?"

"You committed arson?" she dropped her voice to a whisper before saying the next part. She still couldn't believe it. "And killed someone?"

Matt paced back over to the bed and thrust his fingers through his hair. "Do you really think I could do something like that?"

"Will told me everything yesterday at the ranch. Is it true?"

"He's got his facts twisted. I would never hurt anyone, and I'm trying to help you now. Please listen to me. If there's really an insurance agency investigating, they aren't just going to give up. They don't want to pay money out if they don't have to, so if they think there is any way to get out of it, they will hound your family relentlessly."

He reached out and put his hands on her arms. "I know the police ruled it an accident, but if there's any chance that this guy can twist it to work in his client's favor, it can cause a lot of problems for you. After everything you've been through, you don't need to deal with this. I have a friend who can take care of it for you and bring all of this to an end."

Brenna gasped and edged away from him on the bed, staring at him in utter disbelief. "So you won't talk about the arson or the murder that you committed, and now you're trying to get one of your thug friends to 'help' me? Thanks, but no thanks."

Matt dropped his hand from hers at once. "Do you really think that little of me, Brenna? After all the time we've spent together? When I was honest with you about my past right upfront?"

She looked away so she wouldn't have to see the pain in his eyes reflecting back at her. Had she been wrong? Had the P.I. lied to get a rise out of her?

But even if he had, why was Matt offering to have some guy "take care of things" as far as the insurance investigation went? Once a criminal, always a criminal.

"I don't know what to believe anymore," she whispered, wishing she'd never been rescued from that storm.

CHAPTER 23

BRENNA WATCHED AS MATT PACED AROUND THE ROOM. Several times it looked like he wanted to say something, but he kept quiet as he worked his thoughts out in his head. Finally, he took up a seat by the window and leaned forward with an elbow on each knee.

"You said you don't know what to believe. Well, whether or not you choose to believe me, I'm going to tell you the truth about everything, including some things I'm pretty sure you're not going to want to hear."

She stared at him, unsure of how to feel. Regardless of who was in the wrong, they'd already lost each other. That much was clear from the thick tension that filled the room like smog. "Say what you're going to say," she told him, feeling the ugliness rear up inside of her.

It had never been this way with Matt, not before. Was

that because they'd had something real, or was it because he was good at faking it? She didn't know which answer she wanted to hear, so she looked at him and waited for his version of the truth. She'd decide whether she believed it after he'd said all that he needed to say.

"I'll start with the obvious, and that's that you're not being fair to either of us. Ten minutes ago you wanted to leave the past in the past, but apparently that's only true when it comes to *your* past," he pointed out.

He laughed bitterly. "Oh, wait. That's not true, either. Because I've proven to you at every opportunity that I am nothing like your father, that I would never hurt you, that I would have killed that piece of crap myself to protect you if I had the chance."

"Because I'm scared. I'm always scared," she shouted, eliciting a questioning glance from a nurse passing by outside the hall. She dropped her voice back down to its normal volume. "I've always been scared. I can't suddenly just stop because you want me to. It's not that easy."

"Yeah, but it also doesn't need to be this hard, Brenna." The way his eyes bore into her drilled straight into her heart. His pain echoed loud and clear with every word.

"I know you've been hurt so, so badly. What your father did to you was terrible. The worst part, though, is that you refuse to let it be over. You are keeping yourself in that tornado of pain. Nobody else, Brenna. *You.*"

She gasped, unable to defend herself, unable to argue—because the things he was saying were one hundred percent, undeniably true.

He wiped both hands over his mouth and took a deep breath before continuing. "And you know what else? I don't think my past actually does matter to you. I could have been an Eagle Scout who spends my weekends reading to cancer patients and you would still find a reason not to trust me. It's not me you don't trust, Brenna. It's yourself. You're worried about letting someone in so much that you've frozen me out. It doesn't matter that I would do anything to make you happy, that I love you. You made up your mind about me long before we even had the chance to meet."

The room swayed around Brenna as if she'd suddenly been transported to the deck of a boat. Giant waves of emotion crashed into her. Matt loved her. He'd just said that, but it was clear he was now also saying goodbye.

She didn't know how to reconcile what she'd learned first from the P.I. and now from Matt. Had she jumped to conclusions and refused to dig deeper, when all her life she'd wished and prayed someone would look at her and know the truth about what was happening at home?

She'd looked hard and long at Matt. She'd seen him, and still she let her fear win out over his kindness, over her love.

And now Matt wept openly, silently. "For weeks, I've patiently stayed by your side, giving you the space you needed to realize that not all men are like your father. I thought I'd shown you who I am. The person you've spent all this time with is the real me. I've been honest with you because it's what you deserve. I never planned to lead you on only to have you find out later on about my past. I put my past behind me, and that's what I thought—or at least had hoped—you were trying to do, too."

Her stomach was in knots as she tried to think of what she could say to fix this, but a part of her still needed to know the truth behind the arson and the death it had caused. She still doubted him, even though he'd proven himself over and over again. What did that say about her? This man loved her, and she couldn't even offer him the benefit of a doubt when it came to things from that past that didn't even affect her. She'd always thought of her father as a monster, but perhaps she was one, too.

"As for the fire," he said as if he knew she needed to hear exactly this thing. "It wasn't arson. It was an accident, and it wasn't my fault, either. Remember those unsavory friends I mentioned? The ones I never see anymore? The fire was the last straw. They hadn't set it on purpose. It was a cigarette that wasn't snubbed out all the way before making a break for it. I was there, but you know why? I was trying to save some dogs from a fighting ring. I made a delivery there. Yeah, for drugs. But it was the last one I ever made. I saw those dogs ripping each other's faces off, being forced to fight for evil people's entertainment, and I just lost it. I snuck back later that week with a friend who'd agreed to help. Another friend followed. She was the one who accidentally set the fire. We saved more than twenty, by the way. A few died, and it's haunted me every day since, but if we wouldn't have done something, all of them would have died. Every single one."

What? In all the wildest scenarios she could have concocted, she never would have guessed at this one. When she'd made her confession to Liz and Matt in the kitchen, Liz had told her that she wasn't a murderer, but a hero. That wasn't true, though. Brenna had been trying to save herself just as much as anyone else. Matt had risked so much to save a group of abused animals. There was nothing selfish about that. He was a true hero, not a fraud masquerading as one like her.

Matt swallowed and rose slowly from his seat, shrugging back into his jacket as his eyes continued to bore into hers. "By the way, the friend I thought could help you deal with that P.I. guy is a detective with Anchorage PD. His name is Hunter Burke, and he's friends with Liz and Dorian, too, so if you want his help, talk to them because once I walk out that door, I'm not coming back. I hope you and that fear you refuse to let go of will be very happy together, but I can't stand by and watch you hurt yourself. Not anymore."

He paused and gave her one last parting glance when he reached the doorway. "Goodbye, Brenna."

And then he was gone.

Brenna fell back on the bed and covered her face with her hands, but nothing could hide her shame. All he'd ever wanted to do was help her, love her, be there for her. But she'd taken his kindness and thrown it right back in his face. She didn't deserve a guy like Matt. She didn't deserve anything other than what she'd already gotten from her father for years.

Maybe it was time for her to just go back to Florida and face everything. She'd believed coming here and away from her past would be a way for her to heal. Instead, she'd ruined somebody else's life with her drama and ugliness.

Matt had never deserved what she'd done to him, and she'd never deserved his kindness.

It was over now. Maybe she could finally find a way to leave something in her past. Because if she thought about all she'd surrendered to her insecurities, about exactly what she'd lost when Matt walked through that door and out of her life, then the tears would never ever stop coming.

CHAPTER 24

WHEN THE HOSPITAL FINALLY DISCHARGED HER, BRENNA called Kate to pick her up. The two women rode together in near silence, the only conversation revolving around how Brenna was feeling now and how glad Kate was that she and Buddy were okay.

Back at the ranch, she slunk away to her cabin, unable to face Liz, Dorian, or any of the others. What if they'd spoken to Matt? She couldn't bare the additional weight of their shame, not when her own was already so heavy.

Besides, she still had someone else she needed to call.

"Brenna, I'm so glad you called!" her mom practically screamed into the phone the moment she picked up. "I'd heard you were in an accident, but I didn't know any of the details and I was going crazy. Is everything fine?"

She smiled despite her mom's fuss. At least someone still

loved her. Matt didn't anymore, but her mother and sister would always be there if she let them. "I'm better than fine," she said, infusing her voice with every last drop of strength that remained. "But I'm worried about you."

Her mother's voice grew deep and flat. "You know about the insurance investigation," she said plainly.

"Yes, but what I don't know is why? Why did you have to take out all that money at once, and why didn't you just tell me in the first place?" This was the part she just couldn't understand, no matter how long she tried to work out the answers. She needed her mom now just as she had many times before—and she suspected her mother needed her, too.

"What would you have done?" her mother asked, her voice pitchy, strained now. "You were about to leave home, and as much as I wanted you to stay, I knew I couldn't ask anything more of you. Not after all we'd been through already, and even when things got hard with the investigation starting up and your sister getting angry with me over it, I still didn't want to trouble you. The truth is, I knew exactly why your father took out that policy. It was him, not me—and it covered the both of us. He was going to kill me, Brenna. He knew it. I knew it. Neither of us knew when it would happen, only that it eventually would. I had no friends I could reach out to. Your father made sure of that. And what kind of mother lays that type of burden on her children?"

Brenna's heart ached for her mother. As hard as life growing up had been for Brenna, her mother had it infinitely worse. She'd known her husband was planning to kill her but had no way to prove it. She didn't think anyone would believe her. Or that her life was worth fighting for.

"I would have believed you, Mom," she choked out, so angry her mother had lived with this private fear for years. "I would have found a way to help."

"Brenna, you'd just moved out when he set the policy up. You were finally free from the life there, and I'd refused to drag you back into it. Besides, how could we have ever proven anything? Your father had character witness after character witness that all believed he was this great and noble person, long suffering to the women in his life that took him for granted. I had no escape. No way out. He wasn't going to let me go. *Ever.*"

Brenna's tears flowed freely, but her mother's voice remained an odd mix of stoicism and remorse. She regretted now that her father had died so quickly, so easily. The three of them had suffered for years, and he'd only felt pain for an instant before slipping away. It just wasn't fair.

"I'm so glad you're okay, Mom. I would have died if I lost you." She closed her eyes and pictured her mother's face. It looked so much like her own with high cheekbones, a pointed nose, and a mix of scars and other wounds that would never quite heal. "What I still don't understand is why you asked for a lump payment. Why now? As much as I hate to say it, I understand why the insurance company decided to open an investigation. The whole thing definitely raises some questions."

When her mother didn't respond, Brenna had to check to see if they'd lost their connection. But no, her mom was still there, unable to find—or at least to speak—the words Brenna needed to hear to understand all the rest of it.

"I thought about why you left," she said at last on the wings of a slow sigh. "I thought maybe you had the right idea to get away from here. I thought maybe I'd pack up like you had and find some place new. Help you put down roots where you wanted to be, help Olivia find her way through college. I wanted to... I wanted to try to salvage my girls' lives since I'd done so much to screw up mine and not enough to protect you."

Brenna sat on the other end of the line, listening to years of pain pouring from her mother's body as she cried over what she still believed to be all her fault. She needed to stop blaming herself just as Brenna needed to stop keeping everyone in her life at a distance. They were both clinging to the pasts in their own way, and it was tearing them apart from the inside out.

"I understand, Mom, and I forgive you. I even forgive him."

Her mom sucked in a wet breath. "Why? He doesn't deserve it."

"No, he doesn't, but I do. And so do you." Brenna couldn't believe how obvious this revelation was now that she'd made it. How come she hadn't realized sooner? She knew the answer to that, too. Matt's words, while hard to hear and part of his goodbye, were exactly what she'd needed to hear for so long and they were what her mother needed to hear, too, just as soon as she was ready to listen.

"If we really want to move on with our lives, the miles aren't what matters," she pointed out softly, vowing to take her mother's calls from now on, to stop pretending like shutting her out would solve anything when in fact they made both of their problems so much worse.

"Promise me," her mother choked out. "Promise me right now that you won't make the same mistakes I made. Let yourself be happy and give your love to someone who deserves it."

"I promise, Mom. I will, and in a way I already have." She decided not to say more about her feelings for Matt, not knowing how their story would play out, if it would ever even have another chapter.

"And when you're ready, bring Olivia with you and come see me in Anchorage. I like it here, and I think I might stay for the long haul. I think it's the first place I've ever felt truly happy. One night I even saw the Northern Lights dancing in waves in the sky, and all I could think was that my whole life I don't remember once ever looking up at the sky and feeling such peace. Keep searching, Mom, and I'll keep praying. One day you're going to find that place, too. The one that brings you peace. The one that makes you happy."

They said goodbye, and Brenna tucked herself into bed, ready for the hard day to be over. She was determined to live her life by moving forward, but she still couldn't help but think she'd made a terrible mistake when it came to Matt.

"Please, God. Give me a chance to make things right," she murmured before falling into a deep, dreamless sleep.

CHAPTER 25

THE STRINGS OF LIGHTS HANGING FROM THE BARN'S RAFTERS gave off a soft whitish blue glow, wrapping everyone below in a warm and cozy indoor winter wonderland. Paper snowflakes, strings of beads, and glittery cotton completed the look perfectly. Brenna had never been to such a well-organized event in all her life, and she was proud to be a part of it now.

She stood by the food table, keeping an eye on things to make sure there was enough to go around. The Winter Wonderland barn dance would definitely bring in a lot of money for Liz and Dorian's horse rescue charities, which brought her boundless joy. Over one hundred people had already passed through the doors, and there was still space for at least one hundred more.

The band played bright, spunky versions of classic

holiday favorites, and the guests shuffled, stomped, and swayed in their finest pairs of boots.

Watching the couples laughing and having fun as they spun each other around was the only part of the evening that she found truly difficult to contend with. Matt had wanted to escort her to this very dance. And he should have been here, too. Liz and Dorian were his friends first, and it wasn't fair he felt unwelcome. None of what Brenna had done to him was fair.

More than a week had passed since they'd last talked in the hospital, and he'd made no efforts to reach out to her since. Respecting his decision even though it broke her heart, Brenna had decided to let him go without a fight—or at least without another fight. As much as she wished Matt could be part of her new life, it seemed that he was, instead, one of the sacrifices she'd had to make in order to heal. He'd taught her so many important things, and now he was gone. She'd hurt him, and he'd left. She couldn't blame him, either.

Of course, she hadn't realized how important Matt had become to her until he wasn't around to fill her days with jokes and smiles anymore. As much as she loved her job, loved Buddy, and loved her new home at the ranch, she loved him that much more.

And he had loved her, too. He'd told her exactly how he felt, but she'd never get the chance to return the favor, to let him know how much he'd transformed her, helped her, taught her how to trust and see the good in people again—or maybe for the first time ever in her entire life.

With each of these thoughts, she grew more and more uncomfortable in the crowd of partygoers that surrounded her. She just needed a breath of fresh air, a quick moment to herself, and then she'd be ready to get back to work.

Slipping away undetected, she headed toward the stables to give Buddy a quick hello.

But Liz spotted her before she could close the distance between the barn and the stables—and she wasn't alone. Brenna's stomach tied into knots. What if this was another investigator sent by the insurance agency? What more could they possibly want after her mother went on record with everything she had revealed to Brenna during their heart-wrenching call?

"Brenna, this is Hunter Burke," Liz said with a smile that instantly put Brenna back at ease. "He's here to talk to you."

Liz stayed with her, looping her arm through Brenna's for support. "Hunter Burke? You're Matt's friend?" She recognized the name from their fight, the big fight that had officially ended things between the two of them.

"I am. I'm a detective with Anchorage PD, and Matt called me to explain your situation. Can we go somewhere a little quieter to talk?" He gestured toward the group of new party arrivals that swept past them on their way from the parking field to the barn.

"Why don't we go over there? At least it will be a bit warmer." Liz pointed to the stable just on the other side of the pen.

"You can go inside, Liz. I'm okay to talk to him alone." Brenna appreciated her friend's unyielding support, but she also knew this was something she needed to do on her own, that she needed to start doing things by herself, no excuses. Besides, Liz had a dance to host.

She walked across the pen with Hunter, making small talk along the way about the weather, about the dance, about anything except for Matt Sanders.

As soon as they got inside, Brenna walked over by Buddy's stall. For some reason, she just felt safer knowing her gentle friend was nearby. The horse lifted his head from the feed trough for a quick hello, then went back to eating.

"Hey, Buddy," Hunter said, patting the horse on his side. "Thanks for letting us crash your stall for a few minutes."

Brenna studied the tattoo that was just barely visible on Hunter's neck. It reminded her of the first time she met Matt, of what her tattoo was meant to represent. But symbols meant nothing if you willfully ignored their meaning. She knew that now, and she would never make that mistake again.

Hunter cleared his throat before speaking further. "There's not much to say, but hopefully what I have to offer here will help bring you a little bit of peace and closure. After Matt called me the other day, I did a bit of digging into the police investigation that happened the night your father died. Those guys did everything right, which technically should mean you have nothing to worry about."

He sighed, and Brenna couldn't help but join him.

"However," Hunter continued, "with some of these insurance companies, they will keep digging until they've created enough doubt so that they don't have to pay out. And that's what it seems this Will Hardy guy has been paid to do."

"Yeah, and he also doesn't seem like the type to give up until he wins." She shivered in revulsion as she thought about the questions he'd already asked of her, knowing full well he would be back.

"No, he isn't the type to quit. So I knew I had to find something else that perhaps the police hadn't. I called your mom and she told me her version of events that night, which matched exactly with yours and what was put into the police report."

"That's good, isn't it?" Brenna leaned over the edge of the stall to rub Buddy's neck. She couldn't take any more bad news. Not tonight.

"Well, it is, but it won't be enough for this Hardy guy. He's going to keep pushing until he gets something that's off —something he can use to plant a seed of doubt that it was accidental. Once he has that, the company won't need to pay."

Her stomach lurched. How could she possibly prove it?

"But, when I called Matt and told him that, he told me that we had to do something to get this guy off your back. When I told him I was fresh out of ideas, he hung up on me." Hunter let out a soft chuckle as he watched her closely. "He called me back later that night asking for one last favor."

Brenna's cheeks burned as she waited for Hunter to continue. Matt had fought so hard to help her even after all she'd done to him. Did that mean there still might be a chance? And had he managed to find a way to get Will Hardy off their case?

"I got a nice opportunity to play bad cop. Even called one of my lawyer friends in on this. After getting the green light from your mother, we went past that idiot P.I. and straight to the company. They agreed to an arbitration, and in the end, both parties gave a little to get a little."

"What does that mean?" Brenna asked, short of breath from her anticipation.

"It means it's officially over. That guy won't bother you anymore, and based on the terms of the agreement that your mother and the insurance company made, no one else can legally come at either of you or your sister for this ever again."

"What was the agreement?"

Hunter and Brenna both petted Buddy as they carried on with their conversation.

"Your mother dropped the lump sum request and also told them the policy was way more than she'd ever need. They settled on a smaller amount to be paid incrementally over the next twenty years. It's over, and everyone's happy. If she would have fought a little harder, I'm sure your mother could have walked away with more cash, but she told everyone that she was done fighting, that she was finally ready to forgive. She seems like a nice lady, by the way."

Brenna couldn't believe it.

It was all over, this time for good. No one could hurt her anymore.

Even better than that, though, she may still have a chance with Matt, if she could show him just how much he meant to her and just how much she trusted what they had forged together.

CHAPTER 26

BRENNA DROVE THROUGH THE SNOW IN THE PRE-SUNRISE darkness of the Alaskan morning. It wasn't what she'd expected when she first got to Alaska, but then again, not much was. Fat snowflakes fell and swooped at her windshield like she was flying through space. Like so many things did, it made her think of Matt and the time they spent in the back of his truck watching the Northern Lights in the night sky.

He hadn't come on the night of the barn dance, and she couldn't say she blamed him. He'd done so much more, though, by working with Hunter to finally free her family from the insurance investigation and the fallout of her father's death. That was love—not just laughing and kissing and playing—but being there for them in the hard times. That was what mattered.

For days she'd beaten herself up, rehearsing and rethinking everything that she needed to say to Matt. The hundreds of apologies that ran through her mind trying to find words that would repair their broken relationship. Now it was New Year's Eve, and she couldn't stand the thought of ringing in the New Year without at least giving her relationship with Matt one last try.

In almost no time at all, she found herself at the little strip mall where a good foot of snow piled on the top edge of the Pipeline Ink sign. Despite the weather, the sidewalk out front had been recently swept clear and blue ice melt crystals dotted the concrete.

The bell above the door jingled as Brenna walked in. It felt like just yesterday she'd been here for her first tattoo. And it felt like forever since she'd last seen Matt.

"If that's my 12:30, take a seat. I'll be done here in a minute," a familiar voice called from a side room.

She smiled to herself as she heard Matt's voice for the first time since their fight. The buzzing of the tattoo needled started up along with a slight whimper of pain.

Oh, toughen up, she thought, surprised to hear Matt voice the same words a few seconds later.

The whimpering continued for a few more minutes and Brenna tried to place who she thought might be in the chair. It could be a girl getting a flower tattoo on her foot. She'd heard those were quite painful. Or maybe it was a small guy getting his girl's name tattooed on his ribs.

Instead, Brenna stifled a laugh when a rather large man in a leather vest and headband walked out, tenderly holding a bandage to his arm. Well, he had told her it was always the big, burly ones who cried hardest when faced with the needle.

Brenna steadied herself. In just another moment, Matt would come out. Would he actually talk to her or just walk away again? She couldn't blame him if he did walk away. She'd caused so much pain, but maybe, just maybe, he'd hear her out.

Matt walked out of the tattoo room, stripping his black latex gloves off as he went. He tossed them into the trash and pulled out a manila file folder. "So, your appointment says tattoo, but I don't have any drawings in the file for you. Was this a—" He stopped short as he finally saw Brenna standing by the couch.

"Hi," she said with a little wave. It felt like her heart had stopped, like there wasn't any air in the room, like the next thirty seconds would determine the outcome for the rest of her life.

Was he still mad? Could he ever forgive her?

"Hey," he replied simply. "You're not really here for a tattoo. Are you?"

There weren't any sparkles in his eyes like when they'd built the snowman, or when they'd watched the Northern Lights from the back of his truck. He was all business. It was a side of him she'd never seen before, and even though the tattoo parlor was well heated, Brenna shivered as it felt like the room dropped a few degrees.

"Yes, I am," she insisted, walking over to the inking room and plopping down in the chair.

Matt sighed heavily as he followed her. "You don't have to do this. We can talk if that's what you really want." He sat down on his wheeled stool and wrung his hands in his lap.

"I came in to talk, but I also wanted to get a tattoo." She took off her fleece jacket and rolled up her sleeves.

"So what am I putting on you?" Matt asked as he slowly put together the equipment. He pulled down a few bottles of ink and lined up little cups on the tray next to the chair.

"I don't know," she confessed with a nervous titter. She'd rehearsed this so many times in the days leading up to this appointment, but now that she was really here. Now that Matt was so close... she couldn't mess this up. Her performance needed to be flawless and one hundred percent straight from the heart.

"What do you mean?" Matt stopped putting the tattoo gun together and stared at her.

"I've had a lot of time to think since I got out of the

hospital, and I've rehearsed speech after speech and probably a thousand different versions of the same apologies." Brenna took a deep breath and forced herself to keep eye contact, even though it would have been easier to look away as she finally confessed everything he needed to hear.

Matt had his head down, looking at the floor. "Look, I—"

She held up a hand. "No, let me finish, please."

Matt looked back up and gestured for her to continue.

"I know that I could talk forever and not really prove what I'm trying to say, so instead I want you to draw my new tattoo. Whatever you want." She reached out and put her hand under his chin. *"Because I trust you."*

"It could be the worst decision you ever made," he warned.

"Or the best one."

For the next few hours, Matt worked on her shoulder, dipping his needle into various inks as he went. Brenna wished she could watch the work, but it was important that she didn't try to see. She needed to show him how much she trusted him, so instead she told him about the various things he'd missed since their fight.

She talked about her mother sorting things out with the insurance company and the plan to come up for a visit. She recounted the night of the dance, meeting with Hunter, and finding out how much he'd done to help her even after they'd parted ways at the hospital. Most of all, she told him that none of those moments had been as happy or as special without him at her side.

Matt finally finished up and pulled off his gloves. "You can check it out in the mirror."

His voice was still flat, and Brenna could feel her heart breaking all over again. But she'd done all she could, and if this had to be the end of their relationship, hopefully Matt could go on a find a girl that would look beyond his past.

At one end of the shop hung a three way mirror so people could look at back tattoos and any others that were nearly impossible to see without breaking your neck.

There, on her shoulder, was an ornately drawn snowflake against a watercolor backdrop.

Her heart swelled, and she saw in the mirror that Matt was behind her and the sparkles, once missing from his eyes, had returned. She rushed into his arms, ignoring the twinge of pain from the movement of the fresh tattoo.

His arms wrapped around her and she thought back to the night watching the Northern Lights in his truck and to the day spent playing in the snow as he helped her build her first snowman.

"What do you think?" he whispered against her neck.

"I love it," she said. She'd never have chosen this design for herself, but now that she saw how it looked against her skin, she knew that it was perfect.

She turned toward Matt, took in everything about him

in this moment. Which was also perfect and would be one she'd remember forever. "I love *you*," she said.

"Finally!" Matt cheered, lifting her gently by her waist and bringing her lips up to meet his. "I was beginning to think you'd never admit it."

"Well, now that I have, I'm never going to stop. You're going to get sick of me, Matt Sanders." She laughed against his lips, stealing another string of kisses.

"I could never get sick of you, Brenna Barry. I love you so much." He kissed her again.

"I love you. I love you. I love you. I love you..." She chanted, at first as a joke, but then because she wanted to declare her love for Matt at least ten times for every time she'd told her father she hated him.

Hate was powerful, but love...

Love could heal.

Love made the impossible happen.

Love was all she needed to start her new and better life.

Are you ready to read Kate's story? Memories are especially sweet, when you have so few of them left...

CLICK HERE to get your copy of *The Happiest Place*, so that you can keep reading this series today!

And make sure you're on Melissa's list so that you hear about all her new releases, special giveaways, and other sweet bonuses.

You can do that here: <u>MelStorm.com/gift</u>

WHAT'S NEXT?

Kate can't believe she's losing her mother. For as long as she can remember, it's been the two of them against the world. That is, until early-onset Alzheimer's robbed them both of the relationship that had always been so special.

Kate accepted a job at Memory Ranch to keep an eye on her mom, but is left wonder whether she's the one who really needs to heal. Especially as a certain handsome therapist named Jack keeps finding more and more reasons for them to spend time together.

What will be left of Kate when her mother leaves her behind? And can she justify spending time with Jack when she knows her mom's time left on earth is limited?

Join Kate and Liz at this healing Anchorage horse ranch in an unforgettable tale of new beginnings, second chances, and finding where you belong. Start reading THE HAPPIEST PLACE today!

The Happiest Place is now available.

CLICK HERE to get your copy so that you can keep reading this series today!

SNEAK PEAK OF THE HAPPIEST PLACE

Kate Griffin leaned her head against the cool glass window and watched the horses in the pen as they frolicked in the fresh snowfall. They playfully kicked the white powder over their backs and tossed their manes in delight as it sprinkled down onto their necks. Even from where she was sitting, Kate could practically feel the pure joy emanating from the animals.

Smiling to herself, she wrapped her arms around her shivering body, all the while wishing she could be out there with them. Unfortunately, her work in the stables had been cut short for the day when her mother's health took another sudden turn for the worse.

Kate lifted her head from the glass and glanced toward the back of the cabin where she could see her mother sleeping on the bed. She'd left the door to the small bedroom open so she could keep an eye on her mom just in case.

For the past few months, they'd been living together in one of the guest cabins at Memory Ranch, a memory care and therapy center outside of Anchorage. Here, Kate worked as a stable hand, and her mother underwent treatment for early onset Alzheimer's disease. Initially, Kate had obtained the job as a way of checking out the facilities firsthand to see if they'd be a good fit for her mother's increasingly heavy needs. It didn't take long to realize it was exactly what they both needed.

The disease had snuck up on both of them. One day her mother was fine, and the next she was forgetting increasingly big details of their lives. Kate didn't have time to adapt to the news, and her mom didn't have the capacity to fully understand it. Always a sharp-witted woman, the sudden memory decline frustrated her to tears most days. For her part, Kate prayed that the day would come soon when her mother didn't remember enough to know she was forgetting.

Of course, that would mean she'd lost the last remnants of herself, too, but at least she wouldn't be afraid or in pain any longer.

Now that they had settled into the life at the ranch, Kate saw how her mother was receiving the care she needed from the special therapists who were trained to work with people who suffered from memory trauma. And hopefully they could help her, too, as she came to terms with what was happening with her mom.

Turning back to watch the horses playing in the snow, Kate sighed, her breath fogging the window. She let her mind wander back to before everything in her world had fallen apart. Before they'd ever heard the diagnosis.

All her life, it had just been Kate and her mom. Her father had run out when she was just a baby and hadn't been seen since. Truthfully, Kate didn't even care. Anyone who could abandon their family wasn't anyone she wanted to know.

Her mom stepped up to play the role of both parents and had done a phenomenal job. They'd never had much, but her mom had worked hard to make sure they had enough to get by. For many years, her mother had worked as part of the cleaning staff at a ranch in Palmer, Alaska, and Kate had spent many of her earliest days watching the horses and wishing she might someday have one of her own.

Of course, they'd never had enough money to buy one for her—or the space to put one up in their modest apartment. Still, Kate had been content to claim the horses on the ranch as her pets, her friends, and her confidantes.

To this day, she still dreamed of having a horse to call her own, but for now she counted working at this ranch, where she could be around horses all day and still be able to care for her mom, as a massive blessing.

Kate felt blessed for the opportunity, but her heart still cried out in pain at the unfairness of what her mother's life had become. After everything her mom had been through—being left to care for and raise a child on her own, struggling to make ends meet and never taking time for herself—now the very essence of who she was slowly being stolen from her.

And her disease was moving fast, leaving a shell in place of the woman who'd given Kate her everything—the strong, beautiful woman who had always been her best friend, her cheerleader, and her rock.

The doctors had road-mapped how the disease was most likely to progress and the corresponding issues they would face at each stage. However, none of it had prepared Kate for the emotional strain that came with watching her mother forget even the simplest of things or witness her personality changing practically overnight.

At least through it all, so far, she still remembered Kate.

That awful day would come, though. And soon.

Kate's stomach churned in agony from the mere thought of becoming a stranger to the person she loved most in this entire world. She would never be ready.

How was she going to live without the one person who loved her beyond reason and who she loved in turn with her whole heart, too? How could she go on with life when so many of her formative memories—the moments that made her *her*—were rapidly being erased from memory?

Kate reached up to wipe away the tear that slid down her cheek. So many tears had been shed, but the well hadn't yet dried up.

In the pen, Buddy, the beautiful, kind-hearted tan horse, stopped running and looked over toward the cabin window where she sat, seeming to feel her emotions himself. How she wished she could go hop on his back and ride away from everything that was happening in her life.

But her mom needed her, and this was where she had to be. She would give all of herself until there was nothing left to give, and no one left to give it to.

"Kate? Are you there?" came her mother's small and scared voice.

Kate quickly turned and walked to the room. "I'm here, Mom. I was just watching the horses playing outside. Did you have a good rest?" she asked as she knelt down at her mom's bedside.

Her mom sat up, pushing the warm quilt away. Her quiet smile was filled with warmth, and her eyes sparkled with an untold joy. Briefly, Kate wondered how long until that was gone, too.

She nodded. "I did."

They each sighed and then laughed at this unexpected

synchronicity. It had been a joke they'd shared growing up, that their minds were telepathically linked—so similar they were then. Did this mean it was only a matter of time before Kate's memories began to fade, too?

Her mother was the first to sober from this rare bout of laughter. She frowned as she traced the wrinkles in her night dress with a shaky finger. "I'm sorry for yelling at you earlier. It wasn't fair. I know you're only doing what's best for me. It's just hard for me to accept sometimes."

When Kate had been called away from work earlier, it had been to collect her mother who'd wandered outside and was yelling at one of the other guests, wanting to know what he was doing in "her" yard. Mother and daughter had fought as Kate brought her back into their cabin and struggled to explain their situation yet again.

Although Kate had remained calm and kind, her mother's barbs stung deep. She tried to remind herself that the cruel accusations weren't coming from her mom, but from the disease that had taken over her mom's body.

Now that they were both more rested, everything seemed to revert to their old normal. But Kate knew it wouldn't last long. Already the time between bad spells had shrunk at a shocking pace. Eventually the lucid periods would disappear altogether.

Kate sat down beside her mom on the bed and reached a hand toward hers. Her mother, who had always seemed so big and strong, was now sitting there looking incredibly frail —as if her memories weren't the only part of her fading into oblivion.

Even with her reduced capacity, she still loved Kate as best she could. And she tried so hard to protect her from what was coming and what had already arrived.

Even in her worst, she wanted Kate to be taken care of.

"It's okay, Mom. Don't worry about it. All I want is for you to know how much I love you," she said, squeezing her mother's hand and offering a beleaguered smile. "If there's something you should never ever forget, it's that." The words threatened to crack as they left Kate's lips. There would come a time when even this indisputable fact would no longer be remembered.

Kate sat there for a long time, holding her mom tightly as each woman did her best to not let the other know she was crying, both wishing they could keep holding on to each other forever. Of course, Kate knew that someday she would have to let go. But for now, she was going to enjoy every precious moment she could wrapped tight in her mother's arms.

What happens next?
Don't wait to find out...

Read the next two chapters right now in Melissa Storm's free book app.

Or head to my website to purchase your copy so that you can keep reading this sweet, heartwarming series today!

Special Collections & Boxed Sets

From light-hearted comedies to stories about finding hope in the darkest of times, these special boxed editions offer a great way to catch up or to fall in love with Melissa Storm's books for the first time.

Alaskan Hearts: Books 1-3

Alaskan Hearts: Books 4-6

The Church Dogs of Charleston: Books 1-3

The First Street Church Romances: Books 1-3

The Sweet Promise Press Collection

The Alaska Sunrise Romances: Books 1-3

The Alaska Sunrise Romances: Books 4-6

The Alaska Sunrise Romances: Books 7-9

The Sunday Potluck Club

Because nothing satisfies like friendship...

Home Sweet Home

The Sunday Potluck Club

Wednesday Walks and Wags

The Church Dogs of Charleston

A very special litter of Chihuahua puppies born on Christmas day is adopted by the local church and immediately set to work as tiny therapy dogs.

The Long Walk Home

The Broken Road to You

The Winding Path to Love

Alaskan Hearts: Sled Dogs

Get ready to fall in love with a special pack of working and retired sled dogs, each of whom change their new owners' lives for the better.

The Loneliest Cottage

The Brightest Light

The Truest Home

The Darkest Hour

Alaskan Hearts: Memory Ranch

This sprawling ranch located just outside Anchorage helps its patients regain their lives, love, and futures.

The Sweetest Memory

The Strongest Love

The Happiest Place

The First Street Church Romances

Sweet and wholesome small town love stories with the community church at their center make for the perfect feel-good reads!

Love's Prayer

Love's Promise

Love's Prophet

Love's Vow

Love's Trial

Sweet Promise Press

What's our Sweet Promise? It's to deliver the heartwarming, entertaining, clean, and wholesome reads you love with every single book.

Saving Sarah

Flirting with the Fashionista

Stand-Alone Novels and Novellas

Whether climbing ladders in the corporate world or taking care of things at home, every woman has a story to tell.

A Mother's Love

A Colorful Life

Love & War

Do you know that Melissa also writes humorous Cozy Mysteries as Molly Fitz? Click below to check them out: **www.MollyMysteries.com**

MEET THE AUTHOR

Melissa Storm is a New York Times and multiple USA Today bestselling author of Women's Fiction and Inspirational Romance.

Despite an intense, lifelong desire to tell stories for a living, Melissa was "too pragmatic" to choose English as a major in college. Instead, she obtained her master's degree in Sociology & Survey Methodology—then went straight back to slinging words a year after graduation anyway.

She loves books so much, in fact, that she married fellow author Falcon Storm. Between the two of them, there are always plenty of imaginative, awe-inspiring stories to share. Melissa and Falcon also run a number of book-related businesses together, including LitRing, Sweet Promise Press, Novel Publicity, and Your Author Engine.

When she's not reading, writing, or child-rearing, Melissa spends time relaxing at her home in the Michigan woods, where she is kept company by a seemingly unending quantity of dogs and two very demanding Maine Coon rescues. She also writes under the names of Molly Fitz and Mila Riggs.

CONNECT WITH MELISSA

You can download my free app here:

melstorm.com/app

Or sign up for my newsletter and receive an exclusive free story, *Angels in Our Lives*, along with new release alerts, themed giveaways, and uplifting messages from Melissa!

melstorm.com/gift

Or maybe you'd like to chat with other animal-loving readers as well as to learn about new books and giveaways as soon as they happen! Come join Melissa's VIP reader group on Facebook.

melstorm.com/group

Made in the USA
Las Vegas, NV
13 July 2021